ED DECTER

Expedition to Blue Cave

SIMON AND SCHUSTER

SIMON AND SCHUSTER
First published in Great Britain in 2007 by Simon and Schuster UK Ltd
A CBS COMPANY

First published in the United States by Aladdin Paperbacks,
an imprint of Simon & Schuster Children's Publishing Division.

Text copyright © 2007 by Frontier Pictures, Inc. and Ed Decter
Illustrations copyright © 2007 by Simon & Schuster, Inc.

Simon & Schuster UK Ltd
Africa House, 64-78 Kingsway, London WC2B 6AH.

This book is a work of fiction. Names, characters, places and incidents are either
a product of the author's imagination or are used fictitiously. Any resemblance
to actual people living or dead, event or locales is entirely coincidental.

A CIP catalogue record for this book is available from the British Library.

ISBN 10: 1-416-92671-2
ISBN 13: 978-1-4169-2671-9

1 3 5 7 9 10 8 6 4 2

Printed and bound in Great Britain by
Cox & Wyman Ltd, Reading, Berks

www.simonsays.co.uk

For Abigail and Cheryl,
with love and gratitude for the expedition of a lifetime

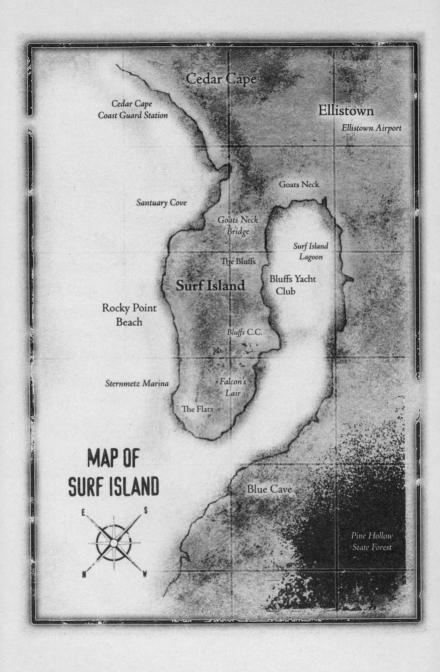

Cedar Cape

Cedar Cape
Coast Guard Station

Ellistown

Ellistown Airport

Goats Neck

Santuary Cove

Goats Neck
Bridge

Surf Island
Lagoon

The Bluffs

Surf Island

Bluffs Yacht
Club

Rocky Point
Beach

Bluffs C.C.

Sternmetz Marina

Falcon's
Lair

The Flats

MAP OF
SURF ISLAND

Blue Cave

Pine Hollow
State Forest

E   S

N   W

THE OUTRIDERS BLOG

EXPEDITION: BLUE CAVE
Entry by: Cam Walker

Just so you know, The Outriders is the name my group of friends and I call ourselves. It's not like a "club" or anything, we don't exclude anyone. It's just a bunch of friends who hate to be bored and don't like to hang around people who do get bored. So we kind of make our own fun, which we sometimes call expeditions.

I found the name "Outriders" in this history book about Old England, which normally wouldn't interest me very much. But there was this one ultra-cool part about these dudes the OUT-RIDERS, who were this band of knights handpicked by the King to ride out to the farthest edges of the empire to deliver messages or bring back people or do heroic-type stuff. And the name just sounded, well, cool.

Super-important Note: This was the biggest thing that ever happened to us, so I felt like I had to write it all down. If some policeman finds this website, remember I'm only twelve and could be making it all up.

CHAPTER ONE: FARMING

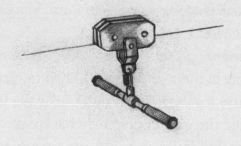

Getting hit by a golf ball hurts. Really hurts. It's bad enough when it happens by accident, but I had two angry golfer dudes *aiming* golf balls at me. I don't know the rules of golf but I discovered that golfers get really furious if you pick up the ball they are playing with and stuff it in your backpack. That's why I was running.

I had been farming golf balls in the woods near The Bluffs Country Club. For some reason, the members of The Bluffs Club never called the trees and bushes around the golf course "the woods". They called it "the rough". But whatever it was called, there were thousands of hardly-used golf balls just waiting to be harvested. Each golf ball (if it hadn't been smashed up too much) was worth twenty-five cents to Chuck at Surf Island Discount Golf and Tennis. Expeditions need supplies and supplies cost money. So you can see why golf ball farming was *critical* for funding the activities of The Outriders.

The angry golfer dudes were now zooming towards me in their golf cart, so I had to sprint to the "guest entrance" that I had dug under the fence that surrounded the golf course. My backpack was so fat with harvested balls, it took some work to yank it under the chain link fence. Once I was on the other side I knew I was safe. The angry golfers were too big to make it through the "guest entrance" and no way were they going to try to make it *over* the fence because of the barbed wire. I scrambled over the edge of the bluff and dropped down onto a hidden ledge of rock that overlooks my hometown of Surf Island.

I guess if you get technical, Surf Island isn't *really* an island, it's more what my science teacher Mr Mora calls a "peninsula" because there is technically a piece of land that connects our town to the rest of the coast. But when there's a big storm (which there is every autumn), that strip of land, which we call Goat's

Neck, floods, and then Surf Island really *does* feel like an island.

The town of Surf Island is really divided into two parts:

PART ONE: The hilly part (where I was standing) is called "The Bluffs", where you find:

1. People with really big houses.
2. New model cars that go with the houses.
3. The Bluffs Country Club where we farm balls and gain access to a bunch of electric golf carts that can be started without a key (if you know how).

PART TWO: The flat part, which is called "The Flats", where you find:

1. People with really small houses.
2. Old model cars that go with the houses.
3. The Sternmetz Marina (named for some naval dude Commodore Sternmetz who died at sea or something). The Marina always smells like decaying fish guts and if you grew up inside

the "circle of aroma" that's how you knew you were really from The Flats.

So, back to the ledge and my immediate problem, which was that The Flats was about two hundred feet below my current position. The only way to get down there was on The Escape Trail, which is what we call the ultra-narrow path that wound around the rock; but it is steep, way too steep to get down carrying a backpack full of golf balls. That's why we installed the zip line.

In one of the rusty piles of boat junk at his dad's salvage yard at the Marina, my friend Wyatt found an old winch cable. The cable must have been used to tow buoys or something because it was really thick and extra-long – exactly what we needed to make the zip line.

We attached one end of the winch cable to this pine tree that jutted out from the hidden ledge (where I was standing) and dropped the other end all the way down to the Good Climbing Tree in my best friend Shelby's backyard (more on her later). At the end of a normal golf ball farming expedition I would hook my backpack onto this thing called a "trolley pulley" and let the pack fly down the zip wire through the trees (all those branches hid the cable really well) and then, when I got down to the bottom of the trail, I could climb up the tree in Shelby's yard and retrieve the balls. But this wasn't going to be a normal day.

Apparently those golfer dudes were *hugely* ticked off and had found some way through the chain link fence (maybe through one of the groundskeeper's gates) and I could hear them crunching through the bushes right above me. All they had to do was peer over the edge of the bluff and they would have spotted me on the ledge. Not only would I be toast, but the golfers might discover the zip line, and that would be *really* serious because it would choke off a major source of funds for our expeditions and get me and Wyatt in ultra-bad trouble for scavenging the winch cable in the first place. At this point I had two options:

Option 1: Get caught.
Option 2: Toss the backpack and disappear down The Escape Trail.

I did not like either option so I chose:

Option 3: Hook my backpack to the trolley pulley and RIDE WITH IT down the zip line.

Did you ever have one of those dreams where you were flying? This was way, way better. I was actually *soaring* through the treetops. It was kind of the same feeling I get when I surf – a rush like I'm on the edge of something powerful and dangerous but still in control, ahead of the wave. (Surfing is one thing I do know a lot about. I'm really good at it. Not North-Shore-of-Oahu-Banzai-Pipeline kind of good, but I'm the best guy surfer in Surf Island. It sounds like I'm bragging, but it's true.)

It was a good thing that the winch cable was so strong, but kind of a bad thing that the backpack's straps weren't. The nylon straps ripped away from the pack when I was midway down the zip line. Falling is a lot different than soaring, so the dream kind of turned into a nightmare. I plummeted thirty feet straight down into a thick clump of some kind of dark green crawling vine. Luckily, this viney stuff (I *don't* know much about plants) broke my fall so I didn't fracture any bones or anything. I just had to pray that it wasn't poison ivy.

I had fallen in an area of The Bluffs we had never explored before, which was unusual because my friends and I had been all over these hills. In this area a lot of the rock outcroppings were covered with a spongy green moss that you didn't find anywhere else on the hillside. Maybe there was some kind of weird microclimate or underground spring that caused it? There was a local rumour that before the Revolutionary War some pirate had stashed doubloons or jewels or something in these hills. In fact, that naval guy Commodore Sternmetz was lost at sea while he was hunting down the pirate. None of us in The Outriders believed there really *was* a chest of British treasure hidden up here, but the idea kind of lived in the back of our minds, so while we were blazing trails or "scavenging" stuff we kept our eyes open – you know, just in case.

Dusting myself down, I picked up my now-strapless (and now *much* heavier) backpack and pushed my way past the mossy rocks, through the thick undergrowth towards Shelby's backyard. We'd hidden an old barrel there which we called "The Ball Barrel" because we used it to silo our farmed golf balls, which is what I did now.

Actually, Shelby (my best friend, remember?) is the most important *person* in this story but I need to tell you about one last *place* before I can get back to her.

BLUE CAVE

Blue Cave got its name because (and this was explained to us by Mr Mora also) every seven years this really weird kind of plankton drifts into the cave and starts to GLOW. Mr Mora calls it "bioluminescent", which is a fancy way of saying it glows in the dark and lights up the cave with blue light. This only happens for like a couple of days in July. I don't know why it happens only in July. I don't know much about plankton.

But the important thing to remember is that this blue glow thing only happens ONCE EVERY SEVEN YEARS. I was five the last time that it happened. I'm twelve now, so if you do the math, the next time it starts to glow I'll be nineteen and when I'm nineteen I'll probably be away in Fiji on the pro surf tour, so that's why I knew we had to get out there *in the next few days* and not any other time. I had to assemble The Outriders and *get moving* or we would miss it all. Maybe forever.

The thing about Blue Cave is that it's about twelve miles away from Surf Island, which wouldn't be much of a problem if you could get there in an older sister's car or on a bike but you can't. The only way to get there is by sea, so you need a boat or a kayak or a para-surfboard, all of which we had "access" to, but of course none of us "owned" ourselves (I'll explain the rules and regulations about why "scavenging" and "stealing" are two different things at another time). Put it this way, it was *possible* to make it all the way to Blue Cave, but first we had to deal with a tremendous problem.

THE TREMENDOUS PROBLEM

Shelby has these parents who kind of think she's better than everyone else (this might be true). Her parents also aren't exactly thrilled about her choice of friends (mostly me). Shelby's really awesome at school stuff. She's like a super-brain. In some ways she's Little Miss Perfect, but she doesn't raise her hand and wave it all frantic when she knows the answer to something (which she always does). She is really into gymnastics, which makes her kind of tensed out because if you fall just once your whole competition is ruined, unlike surfing where you can wipe out and still come back and charge the next wave (which is why I like it). *Anyway*, her parents kind of expect a lot from her, they set the bar high and want her to leave Surf Island and go to a good college. They don't have loads of bucks, so they want

Shelby to excel in academics – which is why they stuck her in summer school, so she could get "ahead credits". It is hard to believe there are parents roaming around on this earth who would be so cruel as to make a super-smart kid go to summer school. Sure, if you flunk everything left and right you could make a case for summer school, but not for Shelby. She could *teach* summer school! But her parents' twisted logic was that if she got "ahead credits" she could take even more advanced classes in high school and get some kind of scholarship for college. They keep telling Shelby (and at one time me, but they've given up) that every class and every test she takes is connected like the "links of a chain" (these are their words, not mine). According to Mr and Mrs Ruiz (Shelby's parents), if you slip up on one test or get a "B" in one class, you "break the chain" and therefore won't get a scholarship to go to a really excellent college. So Shelby who, like I said, is kind of tensed out already from the gymnastics, gets even *more* wound up, which stops her from enjoying stuff like the summer and hanging out on the beach (mostly with me).

Shelby's parents knew their plan wouldn't sit well with me or the rest of The Outriders, so they added the extra-harsh warning that if Shelby flaked on even *one* day of summer school they would send her off to one of those boarding schools where you live in a dormitory. I told Shelby they were bluffing because they didn't have the cash to send her to one of those schools, but Shelby told me her dad threatened to sell the house or do "whatever it takes" for her to get a better education. That's how extra-harsh and evil these people were. So you see, The Tremendous Problem was that at the very moment that the plankton was bioluminesc-ing and glowing blue inside the cave, Shelby was stuck going to summer school and, if she ditched it, we would lose her forever.

Of course The Tremendous Problem didn't seem so tremendous after we disovered two robbers at Blue Cave who would eventually kidnap Shelby's little sister Annabelle.

But I'll get to all that stuff later.

CHAPTER TWO: SLIDING

Wyatt was the one who found the plastic sheeting. He didn't even have to do any heavy-duty scavenging – someone up in The Bluffs just tossed it. The dumpsters up in The Bluffs were like treasure chests of stuff we could use for our expeditions. Wyatt once found a thirteen-inch Sony colour television that *worked perfectly* except for the fact that it was missing its remote control! We donated the Sony to Island Freeze which is a food shack that sells crab rolls (intestinal danger!) and a kind of Slurpee drink called a SurfFreeze that isn't too bad except for the blue raspberry flavour, which keeps your tongue day-glo blue for like a week. Most of The Outriders' meetings take place on the outdoor patio of Island Freeze, except in winter when it gets wicked cold. I know it sounds kind of generous that we gave away a thirteen-inch Sony, but since we were there all the time it was like donating the TV to ourselves. Mr Flores, who owned the food shack (more on him later), really enjoys watching soccer on Sundays, so we earned some credit points for us and my older brother Kyle who is an assistant manager at the Freeze (and who was a "constant disappointment" to Mr Flores). Still, you couldn't turn a thirteen-inch Sony into an ultra-slippery water slide, which is what we did with the plastic sheeting.

I had just gotten back from storing my morning's "harvest" in the ball barrel when my buddy Wyatt (full name Wyatt Kolbacher) had the idea to unroll the plastic down the grass hill behind Island Freeze. The hill was steep, but not insanely steep, and the bottom of the slope kind of levelled out into the Island Freeze parking lot, which was made of one hundred per cent compacted sand. It was as if the hill was designed to be a water slide.

Ty (real name Timor) was the one who figured out how to make the water slide come to life. Ty is from one of those Eastern European countries that isn't on the map any more (or maybe it is on the map but has a different name. I don't know much about Eastern European geography). Ty knows how to speak English but doesn't feel the need to. While Wyatt can't go *five seconds* without talking, Ty can go *days*, which is why Ty didn't even bother mentioning that he tapped into the city sprinkler system using some tools he scavenged from his dad's truck. Ty's dad, Mr Dyminczyk, works for the Town of Surf Island Water Department (TOSIWD). He uses mostly humongous pipe wrenches and monster-size spanners and stuff when he's doing maintenance work on the city sewers, so he wouldn't get tensed out if he couldn't find one tiny Vice-Grip locking wrench and some PVC tubing and connectors. That's all Ty needed to get the water to start flowing *up* out of the sprinkler system and *down* our water slide. The extra added bonus of all that water cascading down the hundred-foot roll of plastic sheeting is that it *un*-compacted the sand in the Island Freeze driveway and created a kind of "crash pool", which Mr Flores seemed to think was a "mud hole", but he was too busy watching a soccer game to pay us much attention (the thirteen-inch Sony, remember?). So for about an hour life was perfect.

Wyatt preferred a no-nonsense "Olympic-luge"-style run down the slide. He stretched out on his back, crossed his hands over his ribs, pointed his feet down the hill, and rode the slide into the crash pool. Since Wyatt believed that he should never be barefoot except within twenty metres of the beach, his basketball shoes got trashed. Having wet feet and socks never seemed to bother Wyatt, so we certainly didn't care (except for the horrifying moments when Wyatt actually *did* take off his shoes and unleashed what we called the "nuclear odour").

My friends Din and Nar (it's OK if you call them the Bonglukiet Twins) had trouble building up a good head of steam on the slide because they were small, by far the smallest members of The Outriders. So the guys opted for a bobsled-style descent down Mt. Island Freeze. Their choice of sled was Ty.

Which brings us to the important thing you need to know about Ty – he is huge. He may even be sixteen years old. We'll never know for sure. At least he's as big as any junior in high school and stronger than any of them. But since no one could find a translator for the school records from his home country and Ty's father doesn't speak English well, Mrs Coleman at the school office just kind of *guessed* and put Ty in our class. So, since Din and Nar couldn't find a bob-sled any bigger or heavier than Ty near the parking lot, they decided to have Ty lie down on his stomach and they took turns being the pilot and copilot of the "Ty-boggan". Needless to say, the Ty-boggan built up a lot of speed. Mr Mora would probably call it "velocity", but the end result was that if Ty didn't *roll* near the end of the run, his head would pile-drive into the muddy sand. Ty and the Bonglukiet Twins discovered this only *after* his first run down the slide. Ty's head (which is very big even compared with the size of his body) rammed into the crash pool and DISAPPEARED up to his shoulders. Being lighter, Din and Nar went flying *past* the crash pool and kind of skittered across the parking lot. They didn't get hurt or anything, in fact, they were laughing hysteri-cally, but they stopped short when they realized that Ty hadn't made the entire journey with them and was now planted like a fence post in the gunk at the bottom of the crash pool.

We all raced over and pulled on Ty's legs, using every bit of strength we had, because not only was Ty hugely heavy, he was *wet*, which made him seem even huger and heavier. Not much happened for a few sec-onds. During that time Wyatt made things a lot worse by repeating something he had read in the Navy Seal Survival Manual (his dad was once in the Navy) about how the brain will die in four minutes if deprived of oxygen, but then we heard kind of a sucking sound like the noise you hear when you open a jar of apple sauce, and Ty's head finally emerged from the mud. He was alive, but both of his nostrils were plugged with sand and he had to wipe the muck away from his eyes before he could open them. We were all really worried about the oxygen loss and Ty's brain until Ty said quietly (he says everything quietly), "We go again."

Bettina (full name Bettina Conroy) who had been "traying" down the hill using one of the rectangular blue plastic food trays from Island Freeze, rushed over and splashed some water on Ty to help clean him off. Bettina and Ty are close friends simply because on Ty's first day at Surf Island Middle School, Bettina lent him a pencil when everyone else was ignoring him. Ty never forgot this simple act of kindness, and ever since he'd looked out for her. I truly think he would lay down his life for her if asked. Right now, Bettina was trying to clean the sand off him, but Ty still looked like one of those Lagoon Monsters from level three of Halo.

As soon as she was sure Ty was all right, Bettina resumed "traying". My brother Kyle (assistant manager at Island Freeze, remember?) should have made Bettina give back her tray, but he didn't because:

1. He couldn't care less.
2. He worships *Viveca Conroy*, Bettina's big sister.

So Bettina glided down the water slide using the blue tray, which kept spinning sideways and backwards, spraying her wild curly hair all over the place. (Shelby says Bettina reminds her of an African-American Aphrodite, whatever that is). Bettina would never even *think* of letting go, being so stubborn and all. Some people think that Bettina is stubborn because she's perpetually tensed out about everyone paying so much attention to her older sister, Viveca. But I think Bettina's that way because she's good at almost everything she tries (like archery) and the rest of the world just can't keep up.

Midway down one of her runs, Bettina heard Din yelling from the top of the hill, *"RA WANG!"* which by now we know is Thai for "look out!" and she saw Din and Nar pushing their dog, Howie the Mastiff, towards the top of the water slide. Bettina made the decision to veer off the flume to avoid being mowed down by Howie. This was a smart move because Howie is MASSIVE (243 pounds!). (I wonder if the word "Mastiff" comes from the word "massive" or the other way around? A good thing to look up on Google.)

Wherever Howie goes – and that is anywhere Din and Nar go – he gets comfortable. *Really* comfortable. He just lies down, plunks his humongous head on his front paws, and basically goes to sleep. Sometimes his eyes droop *open*, so the freaky thing is Howie *stares* at you while he dozes. The question a lot of people ask when they meet Howie is, how do you know whether he's awake or asleep? Nar says he can *always* tell, as he considers himself a "dog whisperer", but the rest of us have decided that if Howie is standing, he must somehow be awake and if he is lying down (he rarely ever sits) he is snoozing.

So it appeared Din and Nar were pushing a SLEEPING Howie to the top of the slide because his position did not change while they were moving him. Howie is so massive that the only way that Din and Nar can move him when he is asleep is to *shimmy* him by moving his front paws a few inches in the direction they want him to go, then moving his back paws in the same direction. Most people would think Howie would wake up during all this activity, but then most people haven't met Howie.

The Bonglukiet Twins are experts at the Howie shimmy, so pretty soon Howie was in position at the top of the slide and then BARRELLING down the flume at LIGHT SPEED. The strangest thing was that Howie did not seem to either awaken or change position, he just torpedoed down the slope, his head remaining slumped over his front paws. Even after the awesome cannonball explosion of water when he hit the splash pool, Howie just remained in his comfortable dog position, his Mastiff head looming above the waterline like a canine crocodile. We all found this hilarious but didn't dare laugh, as Nar might have taken it as a sign of disrespect towards Howie. If Nar feels that Howie has been insulted, he will calmly say, "It's *bpai* time." Apparently *bpai* is the Thai word for "go". Then, against all reason, Nar will fight ANYONE. As I said, Nar is small. He's not particularly strong and he doesn't know any martial arts or anything. He'll just fight. And he'll keep fighting until someone stops him. So we never insult Howie, even when he becomes kind of an *obstacle* at the bottom of the water slide.

Fast-moving water is kind of my *element* so when I got to the top of the slide I just took my surfer stance and rode the flume *standing*. Everyone applauded except Shelby, who just smiled and said, "Ni-ice", which is like the highest Shelby compliment but she had this funny look in her eye; a look I had long ago figured out – Shelby was going to try to top me. Ty, Din, Nar, Wyatt, and Bettina knew that look as well as I did, and they all sort of turned to look up the hill to see what Shelby could possibly do.

"Bring it on," I said.

All of a sudden Shelby *bent over backwards* and got into that gymnastics position she calls the "bridge". Her heels were on the ground and so were her palms, but her belly was pointing straight up in the air. I'm pretty sure a guy couldn't even get in that position (but I don't know much about gymnastics). So anyway, *whoosh*, just like that, Shelby hit the slide UPSIDE DOWN in a bridge position. Not only did she barefoot and barehand it all the way down the ultra-slippery plastic sheeting, she was *smiling*, which looked kind of strange because her face was upside down and it seemed more like a frown. To top it off, when she reached the splash pool she managed to do kind of a handstand, *vault over* Howie and end up *standing* like one of those Olympic athletes who "sticks the landing" and wins a gold medal. For a few seconds there was silence. I guess everyone was kind of stunned and amazed (I know I was) and then everyone started whooping and cheering and Shelby broke out into this huge big smile like she *did* win the Olympic gold medal. I was clapping and cheering myself. Then I lifted up a huge hunk of mud and prepared to dump it on Shelby, which seemed the only thing to do in that situation.

"Bring it on," Shelby said.

So I blopped a handful of mud in her direction and scored a direct hit on her hair, which I was kind of proud of.

"You throw like a girl," Shelby said. Then she started laughing and flinging mud back at me, and since she's extra gymnastically limber, she flung mud really *hard* and it stung.

So naturally I flung more glops of mud as hard as *I* could and suddenly I saw a flash of sky and watched my feet floating over my head as Shelby Aikido-flipped me into the gooey mud. She does this a lot. She kind of considers me her Aikido sparring partner even though I don't exactly know what Aikido is (supposedly some kind of martial art, but I've never seen it in a PlayStation game). So of course I had to scissors-kick my legs and knock Shelby into the gunk so that we were *both* covered with oily, muddy sand. We looked like we had been dipped in gritty chocolate pudding. The rest of the group had no intention of staying out of an awesome mud fight, so soon their own mud missiles were flying in all directions. It was as good as it gets, mud-fight-wise – soon all of our clothes, skin, and hair were coated with dark brown sandy sludge.

Only Howie and Shelby's little sister Annabelle stayed out of the fray. Surf Island Elementary doesn't require students to wear uniforms. But Annabelle Ruiz wore her *own made-up* uniform to school every day. Technically, it wasn't even a "uniform", because for it to be "uniform" it would have to resemble *someone else's* clothes. In fact it was absolutely the strangest thing on earth seeing hundreds of kids wearing anything they wanted to school and one six-year-old girl wearing a blue blazer, white shirt, plaid pleated skirt, knee socks, and black patent leather shoes. If this ever happens at your school . . . well, just steer clear of the freak in the prep school uniform.

Annabelle never, ever wanted to mess up her uniform. So she never, ever participated in water-sliding, mud-fighting, or anything else of a "gross" nature. She just sat at one of the Island Freeze tables and watched soccer with Mr Flores. I only mention this because it is important to know that Annabelle wasn't covered in water, mud, dirt, engine oil and dog hair like Shelby was when their father, Mr Ruiz, drove into the parking lot of Island Freeze.

"*Hola, Señor R*," my brother Kyle said to Mr Ruiz when he stepped out of his car.

Mr Ruiz nodded but never took his eyes off Shelby.

To be fair, just for the record, Mr Ruiz isn't absolutely the most horrible person ever. It's just that he gives off this *vibe*, in the way he walks and definitely in the way he talks, that he's *right*. Absolutely-no-doubt-about-it *right*. Like he has a whole bunch of important information that you don't. Like if you read more, or studied more or flipped through a magazine or something, then maybe, just maybe, you might be able to have a conversation with him, but the point is, he just felt *he* was *right* about stuff and the rest of the world (mostly me) was *wrong*. Maybe it was because he'd won two Teacher-of-the-Year awards, or maybe it was because he really *was* right about everything, but the truth was, he was very *irritating*. And I always got the feeling that underneath it all he didn't like me very much, which might have had something to do with the way I felt about him.

In some kind of freakish alternate universe, my brother Kyle knew *for a fact* that Mr Ruiz considered him lazy, and yet he *liked and respected* Mr Ruiz. It might have been because Kyle was grateful that many years ago Mr Ruiz passed him in Spanish One when all indicators pointed towards an "F" (we all believe that Mr Ruiz passed Kyle to insure that my brother would not reappear in his classroom), or it might have been because deep down Kyle *agreed* with Mr Ruiz about the laziness. Kyle, who was not one to dole out compliments (ever), once said, "Hey, at least that dude didn't quit on me." Which is why, even though Kyle hadn't been in Mr Ruiz's class for four years and was rarely *in* class at that time, he still greeted his old teacher with the only Spanish words he remembered, "*Hola*" and "*Señor*".

Kyle must have a better soul than I do or something, because I was not digging the expression Mr Ruiz had on his face when he called to Shelby and said, "You're late for gymnastics. Let's go."

Shelby tried to look down at her old Swatch watch, but it was coated in mud, along with the rest of her arm. "I've still got time," she said.

"No. No, you do not," Mr Ruiz said.

"I'm not finished here." Shelby was talking about our Outriders meeting which we were meant to be having after we were finished with our water slide, but Mr Ruiz must not have known that, because he said:

"You *are* finished here."

Then a whole bunch of stuff happened that I didn't understand (actually this happens to me a lot).

First Shelby said something to her father in Spanish that he clearly didn't like. Then he fired something back at her. Shelby, if you know her at all, needs to have the final word, so she shot something back. I'd picked up a few Spanish words from Shelby, like *"playa"* ("beach") and *"tabla de surf"* ("surfboard"), but Shelby and her dad didn't use any of those words. So I was definitely lost.

Then Mr Ruiz hesitated for a second, crossed his arms over his chest and said something in Spanish, using his absolutely-no-doubt-about-it-I'm-*right* tone of voice. I had no idea *what* he said, but I could tell for sure it was BIG, because Shelby wasn't able to speak for like TEN SECONDS, which is very un-Shelby-like. Finally Shelby put her hands on her hips and narrowed her eyes and said, "I'm who I want to be."

Because I wasn't able to follow along with the Spanish, I couldn't be exactly sure what was going on inside Shelby's head. But I could tell she was definitely feeling *something*.

For the past couple of years I've had an idea about how girls and guys feel stuff differently. It's not really what Mr Mora would call a "theory", all scientifically tested out or anything, but it is my *idea* that guys have like four basic emotions:

1. Happy
2. Tired
3. Mad
4. Hungry (the deepest of all emotions)

Sometimes "mad" is just an extension of "tired" or "hungry", so technically it may be that guys only have three emotions. But girls, they have like *dozens* of emotions stored in their brains, sometimes three or four of them firing at the same time. Guys usually pick a feeling and stick with it, but girls can flip-flop between emotions several times in the space of a second. And the scary thing is, most guys can't identify what emotion or combination of emotions girls are feeling. It's like a secret level that has no password.

When you surf like I do, you always have to be tuned into the height of the wave. Mr Mora has a scientific term for it – the *amplitude*. That's the really scary thing about girls and their emotions, the *amplitude* of their waves. If a guy gets ticked off it's like a three-foot wave – it might knock you off your board but probably not. But when a girl gets angry, it's like a thirty-footer – you are absolutely going to wipe out and get thrashed on some fire coral. So while I didn't understand exactly *what* Shelby was feeling, I had a hunch it wasn't "happy" and I knew the wave was cresting HUGE.

Mr Ruiz just stood there and stared at Shelby and she stared right back.

There was one of those quiet pause moments that I hate, so I started spraying Shelby off with the hose Mr Flores kept out back of the Island Freeze. That cleaned her off pretty well, but some mud spray might have gotten on Mr Ruiz and his car. Even though he was getting wet, Mr Ruiz's expression didn't change at all, which was either cool or kind of scary. Annabelle had this weird smile on her face, like she was *enjoying* all this and quietly got into Mr Ruiz's car (an old-school VW Beetle). This of course made her look like the absolute IDEAL daughter, especially in contrast to the muddy, angry and amped Shelby. Shelby let out kind of a low *hiss* and ripped open the VW's door. Annabelle made a big show of tossing down a dry sweatshirt for Shelby to sit on so she wouldn't ruin the car's seats. Shelby of course threw the sweatshirt out of the car and sat down, splashing water and mud all over the inside of the bug. Again, Mr Ruiz didn't act the way I would have if someone had just trashed my ride. He just got behind the wheel and turned on the engine, looking forward the whole time. When they drove away, I could see that Shelby wouldn't even look in the direction of her father.

By this time we had forgotten that we were supposed to hold a meeting of The Outriders to plan the Expedition to Blue Cave. The only thing we could *possibly* think about was what Shelby's dad had said to her to cause all that weirdness.

For a moment I looked towards Kyle as if he might have caught some of the Spanish. Kyle, of course, *had missed it all*. My brother was trying to jam the wrong size napkins into the little black dispensers on the Island Freeze outdoor tables. So then we all turned to Din.

Din has kind of a photographic, or I should say

*phono*graphic, memory. He remembers things he's heard word-for-word. Some of his cousins (Din and Nar have no brothers or sisters but there are anywhere from eight to eleven "cousins" at their house at any one time) don't even speak Thai, they speak something called the *Hmong* dialect. (I'm not making that up, it is actually spelled with an "*H*" and an "*M*" next to each other like that.) Din doesn't speak Hmong, but he's learned how to repeat Hmong to his mother, who *does* speak Hmong and she can usually figure out what the cousins have said because Din can repeat it so well. Din didn't know any Spanish either, but he was like some kind of freaky tape recorder so we had him repeat what Mr Ruiz said to Mr Flores, who absolutely *did* speak Spanish. Mr Flores isn't a bad guy; he always pays my brother on time and is actually pretty cool. It's just that he's generally disappointed in my brother for having never made Assistant Manager. I think Mr Flores was hoping my brother would handle the day-to-day operations at the Freeze so that Mr Flores would be free to "think big picture" and concentrate on opening a second Island Freeze in Cedar Cape, but my brother wasn't interested, so Mr Flores always looked kind of sad and disappointed. Mr Flores was from El Salvador and the thirteen-inch Sony was always turned to Spanish-language stations so we decided he was to be our translator. Then we had Din repeat what Mr Ruiz had said to Shelby (the big important part).

"*Dime con quien andas, y te tiré quien eres,*" Din said.

For the first time since we knew him, maybe for the first time ever, Mr Flores smiled.

"What's that mean?" I asked.

"It's a colloquial phrase," Mr Flores said.

"OK," I said.

"'Colloquial' means 'in everyday parlance'."

"OK," I said.

Mr Flores seemed disappointed again. "Parlance means 'way of speaking'."

"Mr Flores? Could we—?"

Mr Flores took a deep breath like he had a headache or something. "That colloquial phrase means, 'Tell me who you hang with and I'll tell you who you are'." For some reason Mr Flores was staring right at my brother when he translated it.

We all looked at each other. If you thought about what Mr Ruiz said for a couple of seconds, it kind of *stung*. "Tell me who you hang with and I'll tell you who you *are*?" It was sort of like an insult about *us*, and even worse it was an insult to *Shelby*. So when

Shelby said, "I'm who I want to be," she wasn't just defending *herself*, she was defending The Outriders (us). There was another one of those moments of icky silence when each of us realized that Mr Ruiz felt we were RUINING SHELBY'S LIFE and in that very moment I decided that we needed to break Shelby out of summer school. There was no way we were going to let her miss out on exploring Blue Cave.

CHAPTER THREE: PLANNING

SCHOOLTASTIC!

Here's the thing about planning – you read about those chess champion guys who think twenty moves in advance or those NASA scientists who calculate how to launch satellites to Jupiter. That's not me. The one thing I *am* pretty good at is figuring out stuff that has to do with real people and getting something that you want. People come to me when they want complicated logistics sorted out.

The planning stuff is all connected with my surfing. When I'm out on my board, I can kind of sense where the wave is going to break, it's like I just *know* where to drop into the best line and catch a good ride. When one of my friends says, "How can we scavenge some rock climbing gear?", I just *see* a way we can do it. And it works. Usually. But this springing-Shelby-out-of-summer-school plan was bigger than anything we'd ever attempted. *Much bigger*.

HUGE PROBLEM NUMBER 1: MRS RUIZ

Shelby's mom is not one of those "oh, whatever" type moms. She is, and I'm using Shelby's own words, "hyper-vigilant". Mrs Ruiz is an estate agent for one of those big companies that make you wear funny yellow jackets. She does most of her real estate work out of her home, so she's around the house a lot. Even when she goes out to show a property, she could be gone two hours or she could be gone fifteen minutes, there's no accurate way to tell. Even when she has to go to some sales meeting, Mrs Ruiz carries her web-enabled PDA, cell phone, and pager, all charged and ready for action. And this is the freakiest thing – Mrs Ruiz talks to almost everyone in Surf Island almost every day! There's not a huge rental market in Surf Island, not many people dream of renting a summer place in The Flats, and no one in The Bluffs rents out their house (they may not even be allowed to because of some Bluffs-type zoning laws). Hardly anyone we know can afford to *buy* a new house, and most of the businesses that are in Surf Island have been there for years and have no intention of moving or "upgrading". So Mrs Ruiz feels the need to constantly "churn the waters" and call her "contact list" (which is everyone in town) to see if anyone is thinking of buying, selling, relocating, renting, upgrading, or downsizing. If anyone in town *was* thinking of doing something real-estate-wise, the first and only person they would call is Mrs Ruiz, if only to make her *stop calling them*. Usually I find Mrs Ruiz kind of hilarious, but not when I need to figure out a way to spring her daughter from summer school. Her reach is far too deep.

HUGE PROBLEM NUMBER 2: MR RUIZ

I'm just guessing at this but I think the one and only reason Mr Ruiz threatened Shelby with boarding school if she skipped out on even one day of summer session is because he *suspected* I'd try something. It (the threat) seems so extra-harsh because after all – *he teaches summer school*! He's *inside the building where his daughter is, all day long*!

*

So, to summarize, Shelby's HOME is in total lock-down, her mom is in constant communication with everyone in TOWN, and her father is patrolling the SUMMER SCHOOL where Shelby is supposed to be. Normally, if both parents were at home, you could pull the medical-exam-with-official-note strategy. Its simplicity is what makes it work so well. You find some medical document on doctor's stationery around the house – everyone has those school vaccination papers or something relating to a younger sibling's strep throat – and scan it into a computer. Then you take the letterhead of the doctor and print up a note saying that the student must be excused for "an annual checkup relating to a previously diagnosed chronic condition". This sounds very doctor-y, and we know it's authentic because once Nar had this weird kind of rash, right where his underwear met the top of his leg. Someone, I think it was Wyatt, wasn't thinking clearly or something and casually mentioned it might be a kind of "nappy" rash. It took four of us to pull Nar off of Wyatt. Nar kind of catapulted off of the sofa and coiled himself around Wyatt's neck like some kind of python and was yelling something that sounded like "*yut diao nii!*" Later we found out from

Din it meant "take that back". Anyway, Nar's rash provided us with all the medical knowledge we needed to manufacture a really awesome get-out-of-school note. But as I said, that requires two not-paying-much-attention parents at *home* which we didn't have. And there was one other thing we were missing and it became the mother-of-all-problems: Shelby.

MOTHER-OF-ALL-PROBLEMS: WE COULDN'T TELL SHELBY

If Shelby knew about the plan, she wouldn't agree to go to Blue Cave. I know that seems weird, especially after what her father had said to her, but this wasn't the same Shelby of a few years ago. Back in fourth or fifth grade, Shelby would NEVER have let her parents force her into summer school. Shelby was always the first one up for fun. She would charge into our expeditions *ahead of the rest of us*. But starting in sixth grade, her parents had gradually started to wear her down. She began to buy this "everything is connected" idea. Shelby was being *brainwashed* by her parents.

Deep down I knew Shelby didn't want to go to summer school. But it was like she was a car on one of those mechanical conveyor-belt things that drag it through a car wash. She wasn't doing the driving any more.

And the sick thing was it wasn't *just* summer school. Shelby's parents had enrolled her in Schooltastic! (The exclamation point on the end is actually part of the name of the business. Someone was paid to come up with that lameness!) Schooltastic! is an "academic enrichment" centre, which is basically a bunch of computers with headphones set up so kids with really amped-up parents can get dumped into a room for four hours so that they can "realize noticeable advantages" when taking standardized tests.

Shelby's parents' master plan for her summer wasn't just limited to getting ahead credits in summer school. That wasn't enough for them. They wanted Shelby to:

1. Show up for "summer session" at 8 A.M.
2. Slog through a full day of classes.
3. Report to Schooltastic! at three-thirty.
4. Plug herself into a program called "Algebra Blaster!" (another exclamation point as if that would make it remotely interesting or fun).
5. Get picked up from Schooltastic! at seven.

6. Eat dinner at seven-thirty.
7. Homework till ten.
8. Catch some sack time.
9. Wake up.
10. Repeat Steps 1-9.

Shelby might not have *wanted* to be rescued, but Shelby absolutely *needed* to be rescued.

So we had to keep our actions secret from Shelby which was super-hard because she's super-smart and can tell when I'm not telling the truth.

SAMPLE PHONE CONVERSATION TO PROVE MY POINT:

Shelby: "What are you guys doing tomorrow?"

Me: "Nothing. Hanging out at the Freeze."

Shelby: "That's all? Just hanging out?"

Me: "Yeah."

Shelby: "Why are you acting so weird?"

Me: "I'm not."

Shelby: "You so are. What's the matter?"

Me: "Nothing."

Shelby: "You're lying to me."

Me: "No, I'm not."

Shelby: "You are. And you're angry."

Me: "Angry at what?"

Shelby: "Me. For going to summer school."

Me: "Why would I be angry at *you*?"

Shelby: "'Cause I deserted you guys."

Me: "You are freakishly insane. Dad's calling – I gotta go."

So you can see why this plan had to be so huge. It was going to require all of the skills, resources and manpower of the remaining members of The Outriders and some *luck*, which was something I never liked to figure into plans because it is usually in short supply when dealing with parental situations. Parents don't seem to know what they are doing, but I find they often surprise you.

THE INTELLIGENCE:

Every good plan begins with research and I had some intel on the couple who owned and operated Schooltastic! Sidney Banston was the headmaster at some private school in New Jersey. When he retired after thirty years, he and his wife Sue (who was the librarian at the same prep school) relocated to Surf Island (Shelby's mom somehow managed to be on vacation that week and missed making the sale) but the Banstons couldn't stand the idea of waking up every morning and not doing anything, especially in a place where there isn't much to do like Surf Island. So they went to this thing called a "franchise expo" which is kind of like a comic book convention except instead of a bunch of people selling really awesome comic books, they sell really boring businesses. Like if you had a couple of zillion dollars you could buy a McDonald's franchise, but the Banstons didn't have tons of bucks (very little, actually. They ended up in Surf Island, remember?), but they did have enough to buy the rights to open a Schooltastic! Technically, what they really bought was a bunch of "learning" software on CD-ROM and some really thick three ring binders filled with info on how to find a storefront and turn it into a Schooltastic! Learning Enrichment Centre. It kind of made sense – the Banstons had spent their whole lives teaching, they didn't know anything about submarine sandwiches, carpet cleaning or overnight shipping, but they absolutely LOVED students and learning. And students loved them right back. They would open a Schooltastic! right in their new hometown of Surf Island!

The Banstons did lack a few core skills however. Sidney and Sue were old-school. Old, old school. Mr Banston wears a bowtie every single day of the year.

Mrs Banston knows all there is to know about the Dewey Decimal System. They treat people kindly, give out great candy at Halloween and if one of their students is home with the flu, the Banstons bring over chicken soup. But they cannot work a computer. In fact, they can't operate anything that is plugged into a wall socket. I know all of this for an absolute *fact* because my father has worked for them since they moved to town. Dad designed, fabricated, and installed the Schooltastic! illuminated sign (that's what Dad does – he has his own sign company). He even tried to steer the Banstons away from the exclamation point. But the franchise manual showed the exact size and shape of the Schooltastic! illuminated sign complete with exclamation point and the Banstons did everything the manual instructed them to do. The day after Dad hung the sign in front of Schooltastic's storefront, he got a call from the Banstons.

"Mr Walker? It's Sidney Banston, from Schooltastic!"

"How's it hangin', Sid?" Dad uses a lot of "common parlance".

"Just great. Sue and I were just wondering . . . how do we turn on your beautiful sign?"

"The switch." Dad doesn't bother to coddle anyone.

"I see. And which switch would that be?"

"The new one I installed just to the left of your front door." I think at this point Dad realized he had the beginnings of a story he could tell me, Kyle, and all his poker buddies.

"Mr Walker, by any chance are you going to be passing by our franchise today?"

"I might be." Our house, where Dad had his Surf Island Sign office, is only three blocks from Schooltastic!

"Wonderful. Maybe you could drop by and take Sue and me through the paces with the new sign."

"Sure, no prob, Sid." My dad hung up the phone and stared at it for a beat. He was smiling.

So my dad actually drove over to Schooltastic! and flipped the new light switch into the "on" position. From that moment, the Banstons simply left the switch "on" and the Schooltastic! sign blazed away day and night. The Banstons had my dad come by to replace the bulbs in the sign whenever they burned out.

After a while, the Banstons kind of *adopted* my dad. They saw him as some kind of "jack of all trades" (which Dad is absolutely *not*) and asked thousands of questions my father didn't know the answers to. I have to say one thing about my dad, he is not afraid to talk about stuff he knows nothing about. Dad was a fountain of advice and counsel for the Banstons. He suggested solutions to plumbing problems, roofing deficiencies, even the placement of flowers in the Schooltastic! office. Some of his advice panned out, a lot of it didn't, but the Banstons came to rely on my father as some type of Surf Island Yoda.

But, freakishly enough, my father did stumble on one nugget of golden advice. Dad knows a minimal amount about computers. He understands just enough to work the signage design program he has so that if someone like the Banstons needs a Schooltastic! sign he is ready. He pays my friend Din to do all the maintenance and servicing on the old PC because underneath it all, my dad is kind of *afraid* of his computer like it has something against him. So, when he discovered that the Banstons felt *the exact same way*, my father tossed in another suggestion. "Hire a bunch of kids from the Gull Bay Technical College to set up and run the computers." And since the Banstons viewed my dad as some kind of electronic, industrial, and general business messiah, they did exactly what he had recommended. My father had no way of comprehending this at the time, but his offhand suggestion was solely responsible for the skyrocketing success of Sid and Sue Banstons' Schooltastic! franchise.

Since they realized that the Gull Bay Technical College students (who later became known as "enrichment counsellors") were going to become living breathing representatives of Schooltastic! the Banstons were very picky about choosing "neat and attractive" enrichment counsellors because they would not only be working and maintaining the computers but interacting with the Schooltastic! students as well. So they hired a "neat and attractive" young dude named Derek Byrnes. Derek is not important in this story at all except for the fact that a girl at Surf Island High had a huge crush on him. Her name was Margaret Folmsbee.

The reason why Schooltastic! has been such a HUGE success in our town is because it is one of the few businesses in The Flats that gets frequented by the people up in The Bluffs. The reason that all the moms and dads in their huge estates would even *contemplate* driving down (or sending their maids down) Mid-Valley Road is because Schooltastic! was responsible for "producing" Margaret Folmsbee.

Margaret Folmsbee went directly from her sophomore year at Surf Island High to this place called The California Institute of Technology. Of course Margaret was some kind of freakish genius and was able to complete the entire Schooltastic! curriculum in like nine days and she was only there in the first place because she was crushing on Derek Byrnes (who did not even know she was alive). But Margaret Folmsbee was technically *enrolled* at Schooltastic! and she *did* end up on the cover of *National Geographic* with the caption, "The Future of American Micronics". I had Din put the word "Micronics" through Google and it has something to do with computers and liquid but I got lost midway through the first paragraph. The important thing is that Margaret Folmsbee knew what Micronics was and she was the reason Schooltastic! now had "enrichment centres" in like eleven different towns. Technically I had never *met* Margaret, but I did sit next to her at Island Freeze one time. I guess I was rude because my brother smacked me on the side of the head for staring, but even when Margaret was twelve and I was five she was super-famous around town (the year before, when she was in *sixth grade*, she had aced a *senior calculus* class). I remember thinking when I was staring at her, "*She chews her french fries just like anyone else, what makes her brain so totally different?*" I did not solve that mystery that day and I don't know what Micronics is but Margaret Folmsbee became the single most important person in the universe in our plan to free Shelby.

THE "FREE SHELBY PLAN":

Since Din was already familiar with and had all the passwords to my dad's computer, we had him pull up the Schooltastic! logo from Dad's files. Bettina then composed a letter from Sidney and Sue Banston begging Margaret Folmsbee to come back and visit Schooltastic! to speak to the new class of students on Orientation Day. Normally, Shelby would have been in charge of a letter like this, but of course she had to be kept out of the loop. But Bettina really rose to the occasion and came up with some great stuff like, "Margaret, you have been like a beacon of light to thousands of young students ..." She got that "beacon of light" phrase from an issue of *US* magazine, in an article about a high school girl in

Dayton, Ohio who started an after school club for brunette girls who "just said no" to dyeing their hair. Also in the letter we dropped in a paragraph about the wonderful enrichment counsellor, Mr *Hank Spiro*, who was arranging the gala event. We included a self-addressed stamped envelope so Margaret could reply directly to Hank. The address was actually mine. Hank Spiro was the guy who owned our house before my dad bought it. My dad and I occasionally still got letters from the VFW addressed to Hank, so I knew that if Margaret responded to the letter, the mailman would deliver it. Also, in the body of the letter, we put in a contact number for Hank, which was actually a cell phone that Din and Nar had inherited from one of their cousins. So if Margaret decided to respond to the letter, only The Outriders would know about it.

We had a slim chance of this "Free Shelby Plan" working if Margaret Folmsbee actually wanted to come back to Surf Island. Here was my thinking. If Margaret was flattered enough by the bogus Schooltastic! letter and decided to make a big triumphant return to her home town, we would wait till a DAY BEFORE she was supposed to come back and print up a bunch more letters on the Schooltastic! stationery. These letters would be to the other

Schooltastic! students announcing this "last minute exciting event!" We would leave the same cell phone contact number for Hank Spiro in case anyone had any questions.

The key to the plan, (technically there were many keys to this plan which made it kind of a sucky plan but it was the best that I could do considering the HUGENESS of the problems I had), was that the Schooltastic! people (the Banstons) wouldn't *know* Margaret was coming until she arrived. We were banking on the fact that they wouldn't tell the most famous student of their franchised enrichment centres to GO HOME. The other thing we were banking on was that the Schooltastic! people had never met Shelby, or if they had, they didn't know her real well. Because we had to slip a Shelby substitute (one of the Bonglukiet cousins) in her place and then reveal our plan to Shelby and convince her to leave and enjoy *just one day of freedom*. All we had to do is cross twelve miles of open ocean, explore Blue Cave, then get back by seven o'clock and have Shelby wait in front of Schooltastic! as she was instructed. And no one would realize she was gone. I know. There were too many weak points in the plan. Too much depended on luck and timing. There were too many variables not under our control. But five days later a letter arrived addressed to Hank Spiro. Margaret Folmsbee replied that she'd be "delighted to attend". It was too late to turn back. The "Free Shelby Plan" was underway.

CHAPTER FOUR: RESCUING

Getting the list of the other Schooltastic! students was easy. All we needed was a very basic distraction. Distractions are what The Outriders do best. We're kind of like a well-oiled team of distractors and Howie the Mastiff is our Michael Jordan.

COVERT OPS

The day after Margaret agreed to return to Surf Island, Nar (walking Howie) and Bettina dressed super-preppy in khakis and a polo shirt (not her usual look of Birkenstocks, painter's pants and camo T-shirt), strolled over to Schooltastic! and opened the front door to find Sue Banston, former librarian, behind the front desk of the enrichment centre. They had picked a time early in the morning when the place was usually deserted. Nar and Howie politely waited outside – you can't bring a 243 pound dog into an enrichment centre without causing a certain amount of panic.

Bettina was posing as a girl (duh) who was interested in signing up for Schooltastic! but needed to set up a meeting between the Banstons and her parents who were super-concerned that this would be the absolute best and most positive enrichment centre she could attend. This was like music to Sue Banston's ears because super-concerned parents and their neat and attractive offspring were the lifeblood of the Schooltastic! experience. Bettina was also wondering if a bunch of her friends at school were going to be taking the enrichment seminar. She'd feel so much more super-excited about it if they were. Mrs Banston immediately pulled out the class enrolment roster for Bettina to have a look. At that moment the door opened and Nar, who was pretending to be very apologetic for interrupting, wondered if he could have a bowl of water for his dog. Mrs Banston took one look at Howie who had gotten "comfortable" at

Nar's feet and immediately dashed for the water cooler as the enormous animal with its eyes drooping *open* looked as if it was in a COMA. Bettina quietly and efficiently took out a cell phone (with built-in camera feature) that she had "scavenged" from her older sister Viveca and snapped digital photos of the enrolment lists. By the time Sue Banston returned, the digital pix had been e-mailed to Din, the phone was slipped back into Bettina's pocket and Howie had been given a drink of water. Bettina then managed to convince Sue to set up an 8 A.M. meeting (her parents needed to do it early, before work) on July 6th (D-day for the "Free Shelby Plan").

Now that the plan was seriously in play, Wyatt and Ty were busier than anyone. We didn't know if we would be able to spring Shelby, or if she would even agree to go if we did, but we had to be ready to set sail if things clicked. We needed kind of a mini-armada to reach the cave. We had me, maybe Shelby, Wyatt, Din, Nar, Ty and Bettina which made seven. Since Nar can never go anywhere without Howie, we had to count him in, but we had to count him as TWO because of his bulk poundage. Wyatt and Ty were our best scavengers (like I said, there's a difference between "scavenging" and "stealing" but I'll explain it later, don't worry) and they had to put together the fleet and have it waiting at a hidden location in case we got the go code.

As the July 6th date got closer, Din printed up more Schooltastic! stationery and Bettina composed a letter to all the students enrolled in Shelby's enrichment programme seminar. Bettina was really stepping up to try to fill Shelby's shoes:

SCHOOLTASTIC!
A Learning Enrichment Centre
AN URGENT MESSAGE:
From: Sidney and Sue Banston, Founders and Chief Executives
To: All Schooltastic! Students
Re: Margaret Folmsbee Motivational Speech

Margaret Folmsbee, winner of the C. Vern Herman Advanced Physics Award at The California Institute of Technology in Pasadena, California, and pre-eminent graduate of The Surf Island Schooltastic! Learning Enrichment Centre, will be giving a talk entitled "How Schooltastic!, Hard Work, and My Dedicated Parents Got Me Where I Am Today".

This exciting event (STUDENTS ONLY) will begin promptly at 8 A.M. on July 6th. We apologize for the early hour but we are respecting Margaret's busy academic schedule. We realize that the date and time may conflict with some of your summer school sessions but this is a

ONE TIME ONLY EVENT that should not be missed! If you want your children to get a glimpse of the limitless horizon of learning and success available to them at Schooltastic!, please make sure to arrive promptly as **NO ONE WILL BE ADMITTED AFTER 8 A.M.**

I don't want to brag, but the stuff about "the conflict with summer school" and the "limitless horizon of learning" came from me. If you knew Mr and Mrs Ruiz as well as I did you'd realize it was kind of genius.

A motivational speech by Margaret Folmsbee would be the only lure on earth that would cause Shelby's parents to willingly take her out of summer school for a day. We needed Mr and Mrs Ruiz to *deliver* Shelby to the escape point. It had to be somewhere they couldn't wait to drop her off, someplace they *endorsed*. They had to feel *great* about dropping her off. And we would be waiting.

JULY 6TH (D-DAY):

By 7 A.M. Bettina and I were in place behind the dumpsters in the parking lot next to Schooltastic! There were these scrubby trees surrounding the back sides of the dumpsters, so we were really concealed. Also, when parents came into the parking lot to drop off their kids for the big Margaret Folmsbee lecture, they would stop directly in front of our location. When Mr Ruiz dropped off Shelby she would be standing not more than ten yards from us. So, as reconnaissance positions go, this was perfect. Except for the gross odours. There was a Chinese restaurant two stores down from Schooltastic! that shared the dumpster. The place was called Island Pangs, which was kind of a lame name for a restaurant, but their egg rolls were really good especially reheated the next morning for breakfast before surfing.

Bettina was the only Outrider that I needed to wait with me. Din and Nar make a lot of noise, and of course Howie is much too noticeable to be on recon. Ty and Wyatt were responsible for transpo. They'd been really evasive about whether or not they could pull together all the vessels we needed. I was kind of sweating it, but I couldn't worry about it until we got to our meeting place on the far side of Rocky Point. So I needed Bettina there for two reasons. She was the absolute quietest one of all of us (she's light on her feet or something – Shelby says she's graceful, but that sounds kind of *soft* and that's not a word you'd use to describe Bettina) and more importantly, Shelby was all tensed-out at me, so I needed her best girlfriend along as backup. For the past few weeks, I'd been pretty much avoiding Shelby and her laser-beam mind. I wasn't sure I had the mental stamina to conceal the plan from her if she started digging at me. So I just ducked her. She knew I was doing this and some of her e-mails kind of indicated it to me:

FROM: Shelby@SurfIslandOutriders.com
TO: Cam@SurfIslandOutriders.com
SUBJECT: My so-called friend?

What is your problem, LAME-O?

So I was really hoping that if Shelby saw Bettina with me, she would calm down just long enough for me to explain the plan. Oh, I forgot. There was one other person with us. A cousin of Din and Nar's. I wasn't trying to be rude forgetting to mention her but neither Bettina nor I could actually speak with her. Technically, neither could Din or Nar. This cousin, I'm pretty sure her name was Puyat, was one of those Bonglukiet cousins that spoke the Hmong dialect.

Obviously Din and Nar couldn't tell their mom what was going on, so they had to rely on one of the Thai-speaking cousins that claimed he spoke Hmong. I have no idea what was communicated to Puyat, but somehow she was with us behind the dumpster and hopefully, if all went according to my sucky plan, she would fill in and become Shelby Ruiz for one day. It didn't seem like there was enough luck in the universe.

You can hear Mr Ruiz's old-school VW bug coming from a half mile away. Bettina crouched lower behind the dumpster; she knew the moment of truth had arrived. I looked over at Puyat whose expression did not change. Maybe she was better off not knowing what all this was about.

Bettina tapped me on the shoulder and whispered, "We still going to Blue Cave if Shelby bails?"

This was the question I had been thinking about a lot. There was every reason *to* go. The plankton were glowing blue, we might even have the vessels to get out there and none of our parents would get nervous if we came home late for dinner as long as we logged in a call or two. Blue Cave would be totally awesome and cool whether Shelby was there or not.

The problem was that once we started the "Free Shelby Plan" the *plan itself* kind of became bigger than *the expedition* to Blue Cave. At least for me it did. Seeing cool once-every-seven-years bioluminescent plankton would be absolutely something I'd remember for the rest of my life. But if Shelby chose summer school and Schooltastic! over Blue Cave, it would feel like the whole expedition was pointless, like we FAILED at the one most super-important mission we had to accomplish. It would be like Shelby chose her parents' plan over ours and that would mean that we'd be kind of losing her from The Outriders. Like all the places we'd been and things we'd done hadn't meant that much. So, in a way, to go without Shelby would be like things had changed forever, and I didn't want to remember Blue Cave that way.

"I'm not sure," I told Bettina.

"Yeah, it would seem kind of pointless without her." Girls are freakishly smart sometimes.

As Mr Ruiz's VW pulled into the Schooltastic! driveway, Bettina and I hid ourselves behind the disgusting, smelly dumpster. I was about to pull Puyat lower until I realized that Shelby would have no idea who she was anyway. Puyat could have been just a

Hmong dialect-speaking girl standing under some scrubby trees behind a dumpster. Nothing out of the ordinary.

Shelby got out of the car and we heard the last words she said to her dad before she closed the door. "Dad, just chill, OK? I promise I'll take notes."

And then Mr Ruiz drove away. Shelby was just standing in the driveway, looking not happy, not sad, just sort of numb. Or at least that's how I read it. The whole point of The Outriders was that everyone in our group hated the idea of ever being BORED. That's what we all had in common – the belief that there was so much cool and interesting stuff going on every minute of every day that there wasn't enough time to waste on being bored. Shelby was the first one ever to put those thoughts into words and here she was standing in a parking lot looking SUPER-BORED. It almost hurt to see it. Bettina kicked me in the shin. I was so lost in thought, I had almost let Shelby get inside the enrichment centre.

I blew my mallard call. I should explain. One time Shelby and I were in this thrift store and there was this duck hunting gear. I'm so against hunters (idiots) and so is Shelby but there was this tube that looked like a three inch long wooden flute that had the word

"MALLARD" burnished into the wood. We started taking turns blowing on it and it made the absolutely worst duck quack in the known universe. So we spent the twenty-five cents (one farmed golf ball) to buy it. Our thought was that we might use it like an emergency whistle on an expedition because nothing in nature could possibly sound like this mallard quack.

Shelby reeled around. She knew exactly what the sound was but it was as if someone had hit her over the head with a frying pan, she looked so dazed and confused. Bettina and I showed ourselves from behind the dumpster and tried to wave her over to where we were. Shelby was so weirded-out by her two best friends stalking her in the parking lot of Schooltastic! that she just stood where she was.

"What are you guys *doing* here?" she asked.

"The Outriders are headed for Blue Cave and we figured out the perfect escape plan for you to come with us," I said.

Shelby's head tilted slightly, like a dog that hears a strange noise. "What? My parents would freak. I've got this Margaret Folmsbee lecture."

"*He* invited Margaret Folmsbee," Bettina said, pointing at me.

"*What?*" Shelby was really lost.

I motioned for the Bonglukiet cousin to come out from behind the dumpster. Better for Shelby to know it all. "This is Puyat. She's going to be Shelby Ruiz for a day. Schooltastic!, the summer school and your parents will never know you took the day off."

"*You* invited *Margaret Folmsbee*?" Shelby seemed really stuck on that point.

I smiled. "You gotta admit, it was the most genius plan ever. Your parents totally bought it!"

"And if they find out that I had anything to do with this they're gonna send me to BOARDING SCHOOL! I'll be gone forever! You know how many ways this thing could explode in our faces?" Shelby seemed more angry than glad.

"I know, but look how many things went right up till now," I said.

"No," Shelby said.

"No, *what*?" But I knew what.

"I can't."

"But Shelb—" I got cut off by a car zooming towards the parking lot.

Shelby had to jump back in our direction to avoid getting run over. There was no mistaking the driver of the airport rental car. It was Margaret Folmsbee. Every one of our parents had the *National*

Geographic issue sitting on the coffee table. It could be no other.

Shelby took a few steps back nearer the dumpster.

"Is that really her?" I could detect *awe* in Shelby's voice.

"Right on schedule," I said, checking my watch.

Before Shelby could say anything, Sidney and Sue Banston pulled into the lot. They looked deeply confused at all the students and cars pulling up in front of Schooltastic! Up until this moment they believed they were having a meeting with the "neat and attractive" girl and her "super-concerned" parents. Imagine their shock and surprise to find THE Margaret Folmsbee, winner of the C. Vern Herman physics prize and the SOLE REASON for their financial success, getting out of a rental car.

I immediately pulled Shelby back behind the dumpster.

"This is where things could go very wrong," I told her.

"I hate you," Shelby said, but without much strength behind it.

"I wish."

"Nice comeback."

"Maybe I should go to *summer school*," I said.

"Shut up," Bettina said and pointed towards the Banstons and Margaret.

We all watched as something unexpected happened. The Banstons rushed towards Margaret and embraced her. That wasn't the unexpected thing. What surprised us was that Margaret held on to the Banstons as if they were THE MOST IMPORTANT PEOPLE IN THE WORLD TO HER. I couldn't be sure but Margaret looked on the verge of tears. Margaret had spent only nine days at the enrichment centre and then went on to conquer the world of big time professional Micronics and yet here she was clamping a bear hug on Sidney and Sue.

"Margaret, we're so delighted you've come back to visit," Sue said.

"It meant so much to me," Margaret said as she released her embrace.

"Thank you, dear, but you would have been Margaret Folmsbee with or without us," Sidney said.

Margaret looked confused. "I meant the invitation."

Now Sue looked confused. "What invitation, dear?"

Instinctively, Shelby and Bettina fell in closer to me. Even Puyat sensed something and pulled into the huddle. If the plan blew apart it was right here, right now.

"Didn't you invite me to come speak to your students?" Margaret asked.

Sid looked at Sue to see if perhaps one of them had neglected to mention this super-important item to each other.

Suddenly, Margaret burst out *crying*. "I bet someone at the University was playing a joke on me. That's what it is, some kind of cruel *joke*."

I felt Shelby's eyes burning a hole in my ear but I refused to turn and look at her.

"Maybe it was some mix up," Sidney said. "We would have never dreamed of imposing on you, knowing how busy you are. And we weren't sure you would come even if we invited you, you were only with us for nine days."

Margaret looked lost. Her tears fell in large drops down her cheeks.

Sue took Margaret by the hand. "Margaret, it doesn't matter. We're delighted to have you."

"I needed to come – I needed some time away," Margaret said.

Instinctively, Sue hugged Margaret again. "Is everything all right out in California, dear?"

"The people at Cal Tech don't like me; all they care about is my work in nanotechnology."

"That can't be true, dear. We like you and we don't even know what nanotechnology is," Sue said.

Sidney was a man of action. "You'll stay with us. We wouldn't have it any other way."

Margaret looked totally grateful. "Do you have a can of Red Bull?"

"No, but we have apple juice and some cranberry."

"Cranberry? I like Cranberry." Margaret had stopped crying.

"Come inside. We even have the bendy straws." Sue began leading Margaret towards the door.

"Do you still want to speak to the kids?" Sidney said.

"Sure, I'd like that. But I'm going to be honest. I'm going to steer them away from nanotechnology."

Sue opened the door for Margaret. "You just speak from the heart."

"Just don't steer them away from algebra," Sidney said as he held the door for her.

Margaret's eyes glistened with joyful tears. "I love algebra . . ."

I turned to look at Shelby. She had been watching Margaret closely and listening to every word that was said as if she was caught in some type of tractor beam. It was as if in some type of freaky way

Shelby was *in* the conversation instead of watching it.

I wasn't sure what she was thinking. All I know is Shelby said, "My parents won't find out?"

"Not unless you tell them."

Shelby stashed her notebooks under the dumpster. "Let's go to Blue Cave."

CHAPTER FIVE: KAYAKING

"**W**e have a problem."

That was the very first thing Wyatt said when Shelby, Bettina and I walked over the dunes at Rocky Point Beach. Here's a list of things Wyatt could have said:

1. "Shelby, you made it!"
2. "This expedition is going to be awesome!"
3. "Cam, you're some kind of strategic *genius*!"

But Wyatt didn't say any one of those things. Here's the thing about Wyatt – if you need a specific task done (like scavenging a kayak) – he's your go-to guy. If you need someone to see the big picture (the miracle of rescuing Shelby) – that's a task better left to somebody else.

"What's the problem, Wyatt?" Shelby asked as she took a mental inventory of the mini-armada that Wyatt and Ty had scavenged. There were two sea kayaks, a two-person open-water canoe and a small sailboat with two white sails; one kind of square and one that was sort of in the shape of a pizza slice (I don't know much about sailing, but I love pizza). All of the boats had Bluffs Yachting and Beach Club stickers on their sides. There seemed to be enough vessels to get us all to Blue Cave, so Wyatt's problem had to be about something else.

"Actually we have two problems. Two *big* problems." Wyatt paused to let the largeness of his statement sink in.

"What *are* the *two* problems, Wyatt?" I had imagined the hard part of the day was already over.

"I checked the tide tables." Wyatt unrolled a nautical chart. Shelby, Din, Nar, Ty, Bettina and I crowded around the map. It's not as if any of us but Wyatt could read all the lines, squiggles and weird nautical markings on the chart, but we all wanted Wyatt to know we were paying attention.

"Our outbound rhumbline forces us to sail into a ten knot headwind with a two knot current. We're going to have to sail close-hauled. It's going to be a major slog."

That "major slog" thing didn't sound good. "Was that one problem or two?" I asked.

"One. Problem two is Howie."

Everyone looked over at the 243 pound Mastiff who had now climbed into the sailboat that Wyatt wanted us to call a *dinghy*. You should know that Wyatt's dad *and* his mom were in the Navy. That's why Wyatt was so nautical and so "mission-oriented". Howie got comfortable in a shady spot underneath the sails.

I watched Nar ball his hands into fists and then say, "Howie is *going*."

I saw where this was headed so I said to Wyatt, "Maybe Howie could be the ballast or something?" "Ballast" was one of the only sailing words I knew.

"That's the problem – he's *too much* ballast!"

Deep inside Nar, a small internal switch clicked to "on". Wyatt had insulted Howie. Nar whispered, "It's *bpai* time."

70

Nar sprang forward and lowered his head, intending to use it as a battering ram to knock over Wyatt. But just before impact, Ty grabbed Nar by the back of the shirt and lifted him off the ground. Nar dangled in the air like a kitten whose neck had been grabbed by its mother.

Ty said quietly, "We go now."

Wyatt looked over at the 243 pound Mastiff in the dinghy. "But—"

"Wyatt, you're the best sailor in Surf Island. You can figure this out," Shelby said as she started to drag one of the kayaks towards the shoreline.

As if by magic, Wyatt's tensed-out expression changed entirely. It was like Wyatt saw the whole expedition in a new way because Shelby believed in him. *This* is why Shelby was so central to The Outriders and why the expedition to Blue Cave would have been kind of empty without her.

Ty put Nar down but still kept a vice-like hold on the back of his shirt in case Nar decided it was still "*bpai* time".

Wyatt said to Nar, "Howie *is* going. But you and Din have to help heel the boat – on my command."

Somehow Nar understood this to be an apology. "Howie knows how to heel, too."

Wyatt was about to explain that heeling a boat was not the same as heeling a dog, but Bettina just shook her head as if to say "*don't waste your time*". She and Ty started to drag the two-person canoe towards the ocean.

I should explain that Rocky Point Beach wasn't one of those sugary-sand vacation destinations you see in travel brochures. For some reason seashells never washed ashore here, only pebbles, rocks, and barnacle-encrusted boulders that lodged themselves permanently in a thick gooey mud that was the colour of tar. The mud also *smelled* like tar and stuck to your feet or shoes, so most of the locals called it "Tar Beach". But I surfed the break here every morning and grew to love the place like it was my own private beach even if I did have to use baby oil to clean the black gunk off my toes before I went to school. I only tell you this because it took some *time* for all of us to push the dinghy (and Howie) across the minefield of rocks to the shoreline and time was one thing that we didn't have a lot of.

Before we set sail, Din opened his backpack and pulled out four walkie-talkies and made sure they were each set to the same channel.

"Battery check," Din said as he gave a walkie-talkie

to Bettina and Ty in the canoe, one each to me and Shelby in our kayaks, and kept the last for himself, Nar, Wyatt and Howie in the dinghy. We all pressed the "talk" buttons on our walkies and heard the loud electronic squawk that meant there were four people trying to use one channel at the same time. All of us enjoyed this tremendously except Din, who wanted us to have more respect for the electronics.

You might be wondering where we were able to get all this really cool gear, and so I guess I need to explain the difference between "scavenging" and "stealing".

What is "scavenging"?

Scavenging means that you take something you need *really badly* and return it in the same condition.

What if you damage the scavenged item?

If you break something – you have to pay for it.

But what if you don't have money?

Then you pay back the debt in other ways. Like if you scavenged a kayak and put a hole in the hull – you might cut the owner's lawn for a few weeks when he wasn't home.

Why pay it back if nobody knows that you scavenged it?

Because if you don't pay it back – *that's* "stealing".

More important, it wasn't like the guys at The Bluffs Yachting and Beach Club actually ever *used* their kayaks. A lot of the members go out and buy the absolutely most awesome 18 foot carbon-fibre Valley Nordhams and then just leave them sitting unlocked in the boat house. Kayaking is wicked hard and for some reason members at the Yacht Club prefer drinking stuff at the bar and talking about their kayaks rather than actually PADDLING them.

I viewed the whole scavenging thing like surfing – a wave rolls in, the undertow pulls out – everything has to be in balance. Bettina called this "karma" but I'm not really sure what that means. All I know was, we weren't stealing and we were headed out to Blue Cave with two kayaks, a canoe, a dinghy, and four walkie-talkies with fully charged batteries. Wyatt hoisted a small flag up the main-sail; it was a two foot square of old sailcloth with letters stencilled in red anti-rust marine spray-paint that said "The Outriders". And with that, we took to the sea.

THE MINI-ARMADA

"SWITCH!" Wyatt yelled.

"SWITCHING!" Din and Nar yelled back.

Din and Nar popped off the port side deck of the dinghy, ducked under the boom and took new positions on the starboard side deck, leaning as far back towards the water as they possibly could – desperately trying to counter the enormous ballast of Howie. While all this was going on, Wyatt, who was manning the tiller, trimmed the mainsail, swinging it back to the port side. There was a kind of WHOOOOSH sound as the sails caught the wind. I finally figured out what "heeling" meant as the sails tilted the boat away from the direction of the wind and Din and Nar were lifted into the air, their small bodies unable to battle the larger forces of nature and a 243 pound Mastiff.

"SWITCH!" Wyatt yelled.

"SWITCHING!" Din and Nar yelled back.

And the whole process repeated again. It was beautiful to watch, but very slow going into the headwind. I now understood the meaning of the word "slog".

In the canoe Ty and Bettina were also experiencing some difficulties. The wind churned up the tops of the swells and made it seem that it was raining even though the sky was a perfectly even shade of blue. Bettina was in the front of the canoe and she had to paddle twice as many strokes as Ty because of the disparity in their upper body strength. Each time Ty would dip his paddle to the *right*, the canoe would surge *hard to the left*. Bettina would have to double paddle on the left, just as Ty would stroke again and send them off course.

This is why Shelby and I were two hundred yards ahead of the rest of the mini-armada as our 18 foot kayaks charged through the wind. I had spent a lot more time kayaking than Shelby. But I had to admit Shelby was an incredible athlete. She was almost keeping up with me stroke for stroke. At first, Shelby would just nose her boat straight into the swells and try to power her way over. Then I caught her watching me. She must have noticed that I was tilting my hips and "edging" the kayak across the swells. The hull of my boat was 45 degrees to the horizon which made it a ton easier to slice through the waves. The next time I looked over at Shelby, she was doing *the exact same thing*. From that point on, I noticed Shelby trying to get the prow of her boat *ahead* of mine (as if I was going to let *that* happen).

We had worked for weeks on the "Free Shelby Plan" and it had worked unbelievably well. The Outriders were all together, cruising the open ocean heading towards Blue Cave, one of our biggest expeditions of all time. It should have been the absolute coolest moment ever but somehow it wasn't.

Shelby was paddling right alongside me, but she was tensed up and seemed a million miles away. It was clear she was thinking more about making it back before her parents found out and less about enjoying the expedition. That made *me* tensed, so I splashed Shelby with my kayak paddle. Her hair got drenched but I didn't have even a split second to enjoy it. Shelby flicked the tip of her paddle and blasted me with a shot of water – a direct hit on my face. The saltwater shot up my nostrils and stung my eyes.

When I looked back at Shelby she was smiling, but a weird kind of smile, like one you put on when the school photographer is taking your picture. I'm the first one to admit I'm kind of clueless as to what goes on inside a girl's brain but the strangest idea occurred to me. Shelby and I were having a water fight but it seemed like it was something *we used to do* rather than something we were *doing*. I know it seems strange, but it reminded me of my dad and his poker buddies talking about fun stuff they did in high school; like the fun was a million miles behind them. The bottom line was Shelby wasn't really into the expedition and it made me feel kind of alone which is a feeling I almost never have and really don't like when I do.

In fact, that's the best part about The Outriders – no matter what sketchy stuff happens at school, or what weird stuff happens at home, you never feel alone. There's always an Outrider up for some expedition or up for just hanging out at the Island Freeze. But now that alone feeling had crept into my brain and no matter how hard I tried I couldn't squeeze it out. And when I feel this way, I'm usually forced to think about my mom.

SAMPLE CONVERSATION WITH MY BROTHER KYLE ABOUT OUR MOM:

Me: "What was Mom like?"

Kyle: "She bailed a long time ago."

Me: "Yeah, I know. That's why I'm asking."

Kyle: "What's the dif?"

Me: "I just need to know."

Kyle: "Nah, you think you do, but you don't."

Me: "What if it's important to me?"

Kyle: "Then ask Dad."

SAMPLE CONVERSATION WITH MY DAD ABOUT MY MOM:

Me: "Dad, can I ask you a few things about Mom?"

Dad: "Sure – hey! How long has it been since we tossed the football?"

Me: "I don't know, a couple of months."

Dad: "Well, we've got to get out there! Toss it around!"

Me: "How come you don't want to talk about her?"

Dad: "Who?"

Me: "Mom."

Dad: "You and me, we can talk about anything! Where's the football? Does it need air? Let me find the pump!"

Then my dad would skitter off into the garage and take a long time digging up the football. After a while, I just stopped asking the questions.

WHAP! Shelby brought me back to the moment by scoring another direct hit of water on my face. I immediately chop-stroked my paddle into the water and fired back a return volley. Shelby must have had her mouth open just a little because she kind of had to choke up some seawater before she could yell at me—

"Stop it!"

"You started it."

"I was trying to make you look."

"Look at what?"

"That."

Shelby pointed her paddle towards the shoreline. A few hundred yards ahead of us was the entrance to Blue Cave but that wasn't what had gotten Shelby's attention. Moored near the mouth of the cave was a sailboat, a thirty-footer, what Wyatt would call a "sloop". The boat had a lot of teak and brass and I could see that the distinctive Bluffs Yachting and Beach Club insignia was painted on the tail next to the name *The Iris*.

"Weird," I said.

"Why weird? They're probably here for the same reason we are." Shelby paddled forward to get a better view.

"Something's wrong." I stuck out my paddle to stop Shelby.

"Like what?"

"That boat."

"As if you know anything about boats."

"I know I'm not Mr Sailing, but that thing is moored the wrong way. It's dragging the anchor."

"So?"

"So, the guys at The Yacht Club may be rich but they're not stupid. They don't like smashing up their own boats."

"You think somebody scavenged it?"

"Or stole it."

"What do you want to do?"

"I think we should check it out."

In the old days Shelby wouldn't have even hesitated, but on this day she did.

"I gotta be back to Schooltastic! by seven or my life is toast."

And there it was. I didn't even know how to respond to her. In the same way Shelby could make Wyatt feel like he was the captain of a battleship, she could also take all the fun out of the coolest expedition ever.

"OK, *I'll* go check it out. You head back if you want." I started paddling towards the cave.

Out of the corner of my eye I saw Shelby nosing her kayak alongside mine.

I pulled out my walkie. "Wyatt?"

Wyatt shot back, "Roger." (Remember, *both* his parents were in the Navy.)

"You got your binocs?"

"That's affirmative."

"See that boat outside Blue Cave?"

"Affirmative. Moored funny."

I shot Shelby an *I-told-you-so* look. I had gotten so many from her over the years it felt good to fire one in her direction. She splashed me with her paddle again, which just proved how right I was.

"Ty, you copy?" (Sometimes I used "walkie-speak" just so Wyatt wouldn't get on my case.)

There was just a quick burst of static indicating that Ty had pressed the talk button. Ty didn't waste words if he didn't have to.

"You, Bettina, Wyatt, Nar and Din keep heading *past* Blue Cave."

"And Howie." Nar had grabbed the walkie from Wyatt.

"Yes, and Howie."

"Roger that." Wyatt had taken back control of the com unit. "We'll stand by for the all-clear."

Shelby and I race-paddled to a small rock inlet about a hundred yards south of Blue Cave. The coastline was sheer cliffs of some dark coloured rock that had lighter bands of colour running horizontally; Mr Mora might have called it "striations", having to do with erosion or something. To me, it looked like the side of a sandwich, two pieces of dark crust with some turkey and mayo in between (a lot of things remind me of food, especially when I'm hungry which is most of the time). Blue Cave itself looked like some long ago giant took one huge bite out of the rock sandwich. The top of the cave reached almost to the top of the cliffs.

Shelby and I beached the kayaks on the rocks, making sure they were totally hidden from view. We both popped the storage hatch covers and started pulling out our snorkel gear (this is stuff we actually bought and paid for with golf ball farming sales. You didn't want to scavenge someone else's snorkel – that would be gross).

"You don't have to get in the water if you don't want to," I said to Shelby, still mad she was acting like she was "dragged" on the expedition.

"You know what, Cam? If you come home late today, your dad won't even notice. I come home late – I'm getting sent to *boarding school*."

"Oh, you're saying my dad doesn't care about me?"

"No! I'm saying . . . just forget it! I'm through talking to you."

Shelby shoved the mouthpiece between her lips and cleared her snorkel tube with a loud angry hiss.

"Nice. Maybe we shouldn't have rescued you."

Shelby pulled the snorkel out of her mouth.

"Maybe I didn't need rescuing."

And Shelby flipped backward into the ocean. She made a point of slapping her fins on top of the water and spraying foam in my direction.

Remember my theory about girls having more "amplitude" with their emotions? Well, I had a good twenty foot swell of anger building. One thing was for sure, Shelby might have been first into the water, but she wasn't going to be the first one to make it to Blue Cave.

Once underwater, I kicked hard with my fins. It didn't take me long to ROCKET past Shelby. I'm not bragging or anything, but I'm a really strong swimmer. The surf at Rocky Point Beach is what we call "chop and slop" and it takes a lot of endurance to push your board out towards the break. So swimming through these swells was a piece of cake, and it made me feel good that Shelby was lagging far behind and unhappy about it.

It was super-easy to navigate towards the mouth of the cave because of the blue glow. I had almost forgotten the whole reason for the expedition because of all the Shelby weirdness and the mysterious boat stuff. Did you ever see those glow sticks you can buy at concerts or the circus? Imagine putting one of those glow sticks in a cup of water, then turning out all the lights in your room. The water would kind of magnify the luminescence and that part of your room would be bathed in a kind of mystical light. Now picture having a blue glow stick the size of A HOUSE, putting it underwater, and having an entire *ocean* magnify the glow. Then imagine that the blue glow itself was *alive*, kind of *pulsing* with life. Imagine how an *entire giant cave* could be bathed in mystical blue pulsing luminescence. I guess I must have stopped swimming and was just drifting because Shelby closed the distance between us and swam up beside me. I looked over at her and could see the awesome blue glow of the plankton reflected in her snorkel mask.

I guess the most amazing thing about Blue Cave was that it made me completely forget how angry I was at Shelby. I think it had the same effect on her because she gave me the thumbs up sign as if to say "how cool is *that*!" I gave her the thumbs up, then tilted my thumb sideways and motioned it towards the mouth of the cave as if to say, "Let's go."

The blue-glowing plankton all hung out underneath the overhang of the cave. Maybe they didn't like sunlight, or maybe there was good stuff for them to eat in the cave (I still don't know anything about plankton) but there was a definite *boundary* between the dark green ocean water and the blue glow of the plankton. Shelby and I didn't want our snorkels to be seen by anyone inside the cave, so we both took deep breaths and crossed into the blue bioluminescence. One thing I couldn't predict (how can you predict anything about swimming in glowing plankton?) was that it was much harder to see underwater inside the glow than outside. I imagined that the glowing microorganisms would have "lit up" the interior of the cave, but they acted more like high-beam head-lights heading straight for you on a highway. Shelby and I were forced to swim with our arms extended in front of us, so we could feel our way through the mouth of the cave. Luckily, we didn't encounter any huge rocks or giant moray eels or anything. I could see Shelby starting to angle upwards for the surface. I could have held my breath for much longer, but I didn't feel the need to show off.

Shelby and I slowly let ourselves drift up and silently we broke through the plane of the water. We didn't have to worry so much about making any noise; the roar of the waves crashing against the sidewalls of the cave pretty much covered any small noise we could have generated.

The inside of the cave was ENORMOUS. Even with the glow of the plankton dancing on the rock walls, I couldn't really trace where the cave ended. It looked like it snaked back a long way. There were those hanging limestone things pointing down from the ceiling that were either stalagmites or stalactites (I made a mental note to go to Google when I got back home), so even if the plankton hadn't been glowing, it would have been worth the trip just to explore the cave.

The other thing Shelby and I noticed was that *we were not alone*. There were two other people inside the cave. A woman and a man were kneeling on a rocky ledge that was set into the north wall of the cave. The ledge was about fifteen feet above the water line and must have had a sandy floor because the man and woman were digging a hole with a trowel and were about to bury an ornately-carved mahogany box. Here was the absolute, freakiest, weirdest, most insane thing of all: Shelby and I *knew who the man and woman were, we knew what it was they were burying and most important of all – we knew that it was stolen!*

CHAPTER SIX: SALVAGING

Their names were Jacques and Crystal Requin. I think it is important for you to know what they looked like because if I describe them to you you'll know why Shelby and I wouldn't DARE let them know we were spying on them.

Crystal was over six feet tall and was hugely ripped. She looked like one of the women from the professional wrestling tour. Her arms were cut, her abs were carved in a six pack, and the small of her back was tattooed with a hammerhead shark. The reason I could see all this from my position in the water was because Crystal was wearing Lycra workout shorts and a matching bikini-type top. Her husband Jacques was much shorter than Crystal. In fact he was about my height but he was about two feet *wider* than I was, and all of that width was solid muscle. There was so much "V" from his waist to his shoulders and so much bulk to his biceps that his arms couldn't hang straight down at his sides – they were pushed out away from his body, kind of like the way a little kid's arms jut out when he's wearing a puffy snowsuit. Jacques was wearing gym shorts and a tank top, and both his and Crystal's skin glistened from some type of oil. It wasn't *sunscreen* it was *oil* and they both put it on to highlight their physiques. I guess Jacques got into the habit during his competitive career; he was a former Mr Olympia contestant and I know his name sounds French but he's from *Belgium* which is kind of like France but smaller. There was a poster of Jacques in his bodybuilding days hanging in the private gym they owned on Pine Barren Lane up in The Bluffs. They called the gym "Athlétique". I know all of this info because my dad built and installed the "Athlétique" sign for their gym (Dad had to call in Din to make the computer put that little French mark over the "é"). My dad really didn't like Jacques and Crystal because they "slow paid" him which means that they took like six months to send him money for their sign. Dad could forgive almost anything, but not the "slow pay". That's why he tries to avoid working for people up in The Bluffs; they tend to do that quite a bit.

Shelby and I watched Jacques and Crystal bury the mahogany box. The thing that was *in* the box was hugely valuable, not just in the *financial* way but in the *historical* way. But before I tell you about it – let me tell you how I figured out how Jacques and Crystal got their oily hands on it.

In reality, Jacques and Crystal didn't spend much of their time at Athlétique. They mostly got paid to be personal trainers, which means they travelled around and helped people exercise at their houses. A lot of the estates up in The Bluffs come equipped with their own workout rooms. So Athlétique wasn't really so much of a gym as it was a place where Jacques and Crystal's clients could buy workout clothes, huge three-foot plastic "exercise balls" and high-end gym equipment like treadmills and stair-climbers. You could get all the same merchandise for half the price at Sportco Giant Lots Discount in Cedar Cape, but I guess for people up in The Bluffs, shopping at Athlétique was more convenient. So, every day

Jacques and Crystal are invited to the huge mansions of The Bluffs which gives them access to all the ultra-valuable stuff *inside* the huge mansions. Maybe their customers had been slow-paying them because Jacques and Crystal had obviously turned to *stealing* and they were now burying the absolutely, unquestionably, no-doubt-about-it most valuable thing from the absolutely, unquestionably, no-doubt-about-it most valuable mansion in The Bluffs.

"eBay," Jacques said to Crystal in his Belgian accent.

"If you bring that up again, Jacques, I'm gonna throw you overboard. Don't you think I won't." Crystal absolutely wasn't from Belgium. She sounded like she was from somewhere in the south, like one of those country-western singers you hear on the radio.

I looked over at Shelby. We both understood that we should swim away, but we just *had* to see if we could figure out what was going on. If anyone had seen us we would have looked like two weird frogs with our snorkelling masks pulled up above our fore-heads and our noses and eyes just barely poking out of a glowing blue pool.

"But she is so simple to sell on the eBay."

WHAP! Crystal cuffed Jacques right behind his ear

just like someone might smack a dog that drank out of the toilet. The sound of the slap reverberated in the cave. Jacques was so overmuscled he didn't even flinch from the blow.

"We're keeping this here *private*, understand? Nobody's gonna pay more for this thing than the old man."

"But if the old man, he doesn't pay, we sell on eBay, no?"

Crystal lifted her hand as if she were going to cuff Jacques again, but stopped herself. Instead, she said, "I made me a couple of wrong turns in my life, but only one big one."

"I am not understanding you," Jacques said.

"My point exactly," Crystal said.

"Ooooof." That was the sound Shelby made when a surge of seawater jammed her ribs up against the cave wall.

Immediately, Jacques and Crystal turned towards the source of the noise. Luckily, Shelby and I had the presence of mind to duck underwater. While we were under, Shelby looked at me as if to ask, "Did they see us?" I shrugged as if to say, "I'm not sure." I motioned for Shelby to follow me and we swam towards the mouth of the cave. We pushed through the border of glowing blue bioluminescent plankton back into the green ocean that seemed so much darker by comparison. When we broke the surface, I looked back towards Blue Cave. I had been careful to swim north of the cave's opening, so even if Jacques and Crystal were looking directly out of the entrance Shelby and I would have been screened from view. I didn't want to take any chances with being heard so I just pointed further north towards where I hoped the rest of The Outriders had found a place to hide.

Kayaking against the current is one thing, but swimming against it is another. Shelby and I had used up so much adrenaline during our original swim into Blue Cave and while we were spying that we had very little left in the tank for open-water swimming. Plus, we wanted to stay underwater as much as possible in case Jacques and Crystal decided to get in their sailing sloop and patrol the area.

A few hundred yards to the north we spotted another giant bite taken out of the cliff-sandwich. It wasn't a cave, more of a big indent in the rock face, and best of all it was almost entirely concealed from view – which is why Wyatt, Din, Nar, Bettina and Ty had chosen it as a waiting spot. Ty and Bettina had "rafted" their canoe, snugging it lengthwise against the dinghy. Everyone was really glad to see us pop our heads out of the water, except Howie, who didn't react much one way or the other. Shelby and I climbed into the dinghy. Wyatt pulled some Bluffs Yachting and Beach Club towels out of a stowage compartment. Shelby and I immediately wrapped ourselves in the striped towels. We should have brought wet suits, we were shivering. All eyes were on us. The Outriders sensed the expedition had taken a big turn.

"So?" Wyatt said.

"Huge," Shelby said.

"Ultra-huge," I said.

"Are we still charted to Blue Cave?" Wyatt asked.

"Absolutely. But now it's a salvage expedition," I said.

"What are we salvaging?" Bettina asked.

"The Golden Sextant."

I never really understood the phrase "a stunned silence" until this very moment. The rest of The Outriders just stared at Shelby and me. Howie kind of readjusted his massive head so that his droopy eyes looked in my direction. Somehow even he must have sensed the enormity of the moment.

I realize I need to tell you a few things about the Golden Sextant otherwise the rest of the conversation

Shelby and I had with The Outriders and all that happened afterwards won't make much sense.

THE STORY OF THE GOLDEN SEXTANT

First of all, and this was explained to me by Wyatt, a sextant is a sailor's navigational tool. It measures the angles to stuff in the sky like the sun or stars and helps a sailor figure out where he is and where he's going. Mostly it was used in the olden days, having been replaced by radar and GPS, but if all the electrical stuff in your boat crashes out, you can still pull out your sextant and use the old-school approach to saving your life.

A sextant is shaped like a big slice of pizza (so many things are based on pizza-like shapes, I've noticed). At the pointy part of the pizza slice there is this tube, like a small telescope, and it faces towards the rounded side of the pizza where there are all these numbers that have to do with the angles the sextant helps you figure out. Most of the old-time sextants were made of brass, but the Golden Sextant was made of pure gold (duh) and also had jewels all along the rounded end of the pizza slice. I don't know much about jewels but there were green, blue, red and yellow gems set into the gold and the effect was kind of dazzling, in the same way Blue Cave seemed when we were underwater.

The guy who owned the Golden Sextant was Mr Chapman Thorpe. Mr Thorpe had the biggest house in The Bluffs, and also the oldest. Most of the houses up in The Bluffs are made out of some combination of wood and stone but Mr Thorpe's house was made *entirely* of stone and looked more like a small English castle, though I've never been to England so I really can't say for sure. The main thing was it reminded everyone of a castle and nobody in town even called it a house; they referred to it as an "estate". It wasn't just that Mr Thorpe had a lot of money, which of course he had buckets and buckets of, but his family had been around this area for like *centuries*. For instance, it was his great-grandfather who founded and built The Bluffs Country Club. As if that wasn't enough, Mr Thorpe's grandfather founded and built The Bluffs Yachting and Beach Club. In fact everything that is now The Bluffs used to all be part of the original Thorpe estate which one of the super-old-time Thorpes had gotten as a gift from the KING OF ENGLAND!

Mr Chapman Thorpe (rumour had it his friends

called him "Chappy" but I certainly didn't know anyone who did) was a very old dude, maybe seventy-five, and had trouble walking. Something happened to his legs when he was a kid and he has to use these weird-looking metal canes to move around.

I bet you're thinking it's odd that a twelve-year-old kid from The Flats (me) knows so much about a big important guy like Mr Thorpe. But the thing is I've been to his estate! In fact every sixth grader in Surf Island has been to "Falcon's Lair" (his house has a *name*! No street number!). You see Mr Thorpe didn't actually work a regular job or anything. He spent all his time collecting olden stuff, which he called "antiquities". He was kind of obsessed with historical-type stuff, particularly antiquities relating to his family. When you reached sixth grade at Surf Island Elementary, the first field trip of the year was to "Falcon's Lair". After the school bus went through the front gates of the estate and drove down this long, long driveway (like a *mile*) you got out and – here's the freaky part – Mr Chapman Thorpe was standing there (with his canes) to greet you! He actually shook the hand of every sixth grader at Surf Island Elementary! He even seemed enthusiastic about it. Then he *personally* would lead us on a tour through his mansion telling us about all the olden stuff, piece by piece. He was the person who relayed the rumours about pirate treasure buried in a secret location somewhere in The Bluffs and he was the guy who told us all about Commodore Sternmetz who was lost at sea trying to find the pirate who buried the treasure. In fact, the centrepiece of Mr Thorpe's collection was the Golden Sextant which was salvaged directly from the wreck of Commodore Sternmetz's schooner. The sextant had been a gift to the Commodore from the King of England, and apparently it was more for "show" than daily use. Sternmetz used a normal brass sextant to navigate to the New World and kept the golden one in a mahogany box; the same box I saw Jacques and Crystal burying. Mr Thorpe needed to get some exercise (for his bad legs) and so he had hired Jacques and Crystal to come to his house every day. So it wasn't very difficult to figure out *how* Jacques and Crystal got their hands on the treasure, and *who* they intended to ransom it to. And it wasn't even that difficult to come up with a plan to dig up the mahogany box and return the Golden Sextant to Mr Thorpe.

THE PLAN TO RETURN THE GOLDEN SEXTANT

The first thing we did was have Bettina post a lookout position. Bettina is a super-good rock climber, being so graceful and all, and she scrambled up the rock wall above the inlet using only tiny footholds and crevices. From her vantage point Bettina could see the mouth to Blue Cave and would be able to alert us if and when Jacques and Crystal boarded their sloop (which Wyatt explained actually belonged to Mr Thorpe). If Jacques and Crystal sailed *south*, then we'd simply wait till they were out of sight and then navigate the mini-armada to Blue Cave, dig up the Golden Sextant, sail back to Surf Island and return the priceless treasure to Mr Thorpe. If Jacques and Crystal decided to sail *north*, we had big problems. The indent we were hiding in would provide no cover if the trainers sailed in our direction. Also, Mr Thorpe's sloop *The Iris* was much bigger and much faster than the canoe and dinghy (our kayaks were beached back to the *south* of Blue Cave, remember?) and the sloop wasn't over-ballasted with a 243 pound Mastiff. If Jacques and Crystal came our way, we planned to scatter and who-ever made it back to Surf Island first would send help for the others. Again, it was a pretty sucky plan, but the only one available to us at the moment.

A rock plopped into the water alongside the dinghy. We looked up to see Bettina silently motioning that the sloop was now sailing – and it was heading *south*. We were all deeply relieved and started getting the dinghy and the canoe ready for the short trip back to Blue Cave. We all looked up towards Bettina who had her gaze focused on the sails of *The Iris*. Besides being the best climber, Bettina probably had the best eyesight of any of us – the archery made her really target-focused. If Bettina couldn't see the sails of *The Iris* any more, none of us could. When she gave us the all clear signal, we knew the boat was absolutely gone.

The trip back to Blue Cave only took a few minutes because for the first time we were travelling *with* the wind and the current.

When Wyatt, Bettina, Din, Nar and Ty entered Blue Cave for the first time, I got a chance to experience that stunned silence thing for a second time. They were *awed* by how cool it was. I wasn't even bothered that Shelby was checking her Swatch to see if we had enough time to make it back to Schooltastic! The blown-away expressions on the rest of The Outriders' faces had totally justified all the time and effort we put into getting here. And on top of everything else, we were digging up a buried treasure and "pirating" it back to the rightful owner. Nothing could be cooler than that.

Wyatt had this little folding shovel which he insisted on calling an "entrenching tool" and in about two minutes we had unearthed the mahogany box. Just to be sure nothing had happened to the contents we opened the latch, lifted the lid – and there it was – the Golden Sextant. It's kind of hard to describe what it was like to see the gold and jewels of the sextant glowing in the blue bioluminescence inside the cave. I'll just say we had a third moment of stunned silence. None of us even tried to touch or pick up the sextant; that was the kind of respect we had for it.

Wyatt made a big deal of stowing the mahogany box inside the dinghy. Being so nautical and gear-oriented, Wyatt had brought along a bunch of bungee cords. He even convinced Din and Nar to shimmy Howie into a more forward position inside the boat to make room for the box. Wyatt also took the precaution of strapping two lifejackets around the outside of the mahogany box so that even if the dinghy was torpedoed by an enemy submarine, the Golden Sextant would be washed ashore on some beach unharmed.

We sailed briefly to the rock cove where Shelby and I had hidden the kayaks. Once back in our ultra-high-end Valley Nordham, Shelby and I pulled into formation with the dinghy and the canoe; no one wanted to take the chance of being separated now that we were transporting such valuable cargo.

It's interesting how the same thought can pop into the heads of a bunch of different people at the same time. I think it was Din who said the thought out loud – "What if Mr Thorpe gives us a reward?"

Everyone thought about this for a moment. I knew for a fact Ty couldn't care less about a reward one way or the other. I'm not sure what his life was like in that Eastern European country he came from (he never spoke about it) but it always seemed to me that the only thing Ty really cared about was being with The Outriders. Of course he never really talked about that either, but it was clear because he was never anywhere *without* us. But Shelby, Wyatt, Bettina, Din, Nar and I must not have been as pure or unselfish as Ty because we were absolutely think-ing about a reward.

"You think it might be like a hundred dollars?" Wyatt said.

"A *hundred*? More like a *thousand*. Don't you know

how valuable this thing is?" Din tapped on the mahogany box as he spoke.

"Maybe he'll give us a lifetime supply of steak!" Nar said as Howie's ear flinched in his master's direction.

"Or let us live in his mansion," Bettina said. Bettina and her ultra-gorgeous sister Viveca lived in a small apartment above The Cut Hut, the hair salon place their mother and father ran. Bettina was always imagining cool places to live that weren't her apartment.

"How will Mr Thorpe know we didn't steal it ourselves and then bring it back just to collect a reward?" Shelby's question hit us like a cold spray of sea foam in the face.

My brain had already gone there and I already knew how I wanted to handle the whole thing. "He'll know we didn't steal it because we're not going to ask for any reward and we're not going to take any if he offers it."

"We're *not* going to take a reward?" Wyatt said.

"Even if he offers it?" Din's face was all scrunched-up with confusion.

"It's the only move," I said. "If we don't ask for anything, and don't take anything, then two things will happen. The first is that Mr Thorpe will *know* we didn't steal the sextant. And the second is the most important – Mr Thorpe will *owe* us."

The group thought this over for a moment.

"Owe us *what*?" Bettina said.

"I have no idea."

"I don't get it," Wyatt said. As I mentioned, big picture thinking wasn't his strongpoint.

"Mr Thorpe owing us a favour is way huger and more powerful than each of us walking away with a hundred bucks," I said, knowing exactly how *huge* a hundred dollars would be to each of us.

"How come?" Nar now looked as confused as his brother.

"We'll each spend the hundred, maybe on some gear or other dumb stuff. The money will last a couple of months at most; but Mr Thorpe owing us – that lasts forever. Everyone up in The Bluffs will know that we were the kids from The Flats who rescued the sextant *and didn't ask for a thing*. We'll gain some cred with a bunch of people who kind of look down on us at the moment."

I couldn't help but notice the Bluffs Yachting and Beach Club stickers on the side of my scavenged kayak. The whole group was staring at me now and I was hoping that I wasn't leading us all into a huge mistake. The Outriders look to me to kind of be the planner and the leader and so a lot of times I feel *pressure* to back up their faith in me.

"Do we ever cash in on Mr Thorpe owing us?" Din asked.

"Maybe later, when it's something huge. Like with Shelby."

Shelby looked over at me. She had no idea how she was part of my grand concept.

"Shelby's parents want her to end up at some ultra-intense college, right? Well, I'm not sure how somebody actually ends up at one of those places, but you can bet your life that Mr Thorpe knows how. So even if it's a couple of years down the line – that's the type of thing that's worth cashing in on."

I couldn't read Shelby's expression at that moment. I just know that what I said had some kind of *impact* on her. I didn't know if she was kind of angry, kind of confused, or kind of hungry, but she said, "Hey, I don't want this whole thing to be about *me*."

"This whole day. About you." Ty had finally spoken.

Shelby looked all tensed-out. Once again, I couldn't figure out exactly why. Didn't she know that the "Free Shelby Plan" had become far more important than the "Expedition to Blue Cave"?

"We do as Cam," Ty said. And that was that. Shelby, Wyatt, Bettina, Din and Nar were not going to even dream of asking Mr Thorpe for a reward. I do a lot of talking, but everyone seems to really *listen* to Ty.

The dinghy's sails were full of wind, the canoe and the kayaks were slicing effortlessly through the waves and our hold was full of stolen treasure dug up in a blue-glowing cave. You can lie in your bed at night and dream of ultra-cool stuff you'd like to be doing, but none of those dreams could match how it felt to be sailing back towards Surf Island at that moment. The only thing that could have made it better was if we hadn't been spotted by Jacques and Crystal.

CHAPTER SEVEN: RETURNING

Bettina's sister, Viveca, is really, really, really beautiful. Bettina's hair is curly and wild but Viveca's is super-straight and kind of glossy. She's always doing something with it – hooking it behind her ears or gently flicking it away from her face and she must use some kind of special shampoo because her hair smells really, really, really good. Don't get me wrong, it's not like I'm crushing on her, she's way too old (19). It's just that every guy anywhere near her age (including my brother Kyle) seems to get really goofy when Viveca is around. Kyle has given Viveca in excess of nine thousand free SurfFreezes. Every time

Kyle says to Viveca, "this one's on the house," Viveca does this kind of breathy inhale, like she's *absolutely shocked and delighted*. Then she kind of tilts her chin downward which causes that glossy hair of hers to casually drape across her face like she's about to tell the most amazing secret. She looks right at my brother and says, "Kyle, thank you *sooo* much." My brother looks so forward to this thrilling moment that he is absolutely *terrified* to risk destroying it by asking Viveca out. Deep down, Kyle must know that he is not fated to be Viveca Conroy's boyfriend, mainly because Viveca will date only much *older* guys who are gainfully employed and drive late-model cars or pickups. And for that reason, Viveca was one of the most important *associates* of The Outriders.

Bettina and her sister were not especially close, in fact Bettina resented the two or three hours per day that Viveca spent using make-up and hair products in the one bathroom at the tiny Conroy apartment. But while the sisters did not have a tight bond they *did* have an understanding. You see, Viveca didn't just date one older-guy-with-a-nice-car at a time. She dated a whole bunch of them at once – and none of them knew about the others. The only person on earth who knew the full scope of Viveca's multifaceted social life was Bettina. And Bettina was wicked-good at keeping a secret. She could withstand any type of parental interrogation that Mr and Mrs Conroy could dish out. So in return for Bettina's silence, Viveca was willing (on a limited basis) to help us out from time to time, especially when we were in need of a vehicle that required a driver's licence. That's why, when our mini-armada got back to Sternmetz Marina at about three-thirty in the afternoon, there was a guy named Ernie Driscoll waiting behind the wheel of his brand new Dodge Ram pickup with Viveca Conroy in the passenger seat by his side.

Bettina had set this all up by cell phone while we were still out at sea. One of Din's cousins had given him this awesome PDA phone; it was so full-featured that even Din was having difficulty finding ways to use all of the powerful pre-installed software. Din's PDA could hook up to the Internet, display full-motion video and connect to multi-player games although Din refused to take advantage of this last feature because he insisted it chewed up too much battery life. The absolute ultra-coolest thing about the phone was that we didn't have to pay for it. No one did. Din's cousin was some kind of electronics genius and had worked some magic with the phone's "transponder chip". I am pretty sure (positive actually) that Din's cousin had broken the law by tampering with the phone. Our first clue that everything was not on the up and up was that Din got the phone shipped to him in an unmarked box containing an old pair of Nike Air Jordan basketball shoes. The actual handset was wrapped in some tube socks and stuffed into the right high top. Now I know I went into great detail about the differences between "scavenging" and "stealing". Din's cousin might have been the dude who "modified" the phone, but we were the people who were *using* it. Technically, we were *stealing* by using the phone. But I have to be honest, it didn't *feel* like stealing; it felt like winning the lottery. Bettina claimed that we were all inviting bad karma if we used the phone. We all agreed, but not one of us would stop using it, including Bettina. I guess there are dark hidden parts to the human soul and all it takes are free cellular minutes to drag them into the light.

Anyway, Din lent what he calls the "Bahtphone" (*Baht* means "shoe" in Thai which is funny because of how the phone was delivered) to Bettina, she called her sister Viveca and that is why Ernie and Viveca were waiting for us at the Marina with a blanket in the truck bed.

We needed the truck to transport us all up the hill to The Bluffs and deliver the Golden Sextant to Mr Thorpe. We needed the blanket to conceal Shelby in case her mom was cruising around in her car trying to churn up some real estate business. The winds on our return trip had completely dried us off. Amazingly, we still had plenty of time to become treasure-returning heroes and still get Shelby back to Schooltastic! so she wouldn't be busted by her parents.

We had a small delay when Howie hopped into the back of the pickup and immediately made himself "comfortable" on top of the blanket that was brought to conceal Shelby. It was a natural assumption for Howie to believe that he should get the blanket, but it took Din and Nar ten full minutes to coax him to give it up. The rest of The Outriders then piled into the truck bed and Ernie drove out of the Marina towards Mid-Valley Road and the ascent towards Falcon's Lair.

Some of you may be thinking – "Seven kids and a dog in the back of a pickup truck with no *seatbelts*?"

MY THOUGHTS ON SAFETY

Safety is absolutely important. But if you make a full-time career of worrying about safety, you'd probably never get out of bed in the morning. It's kind of like Shelby and her parents. Shelby is the best student of all of us (by far) and yet her parents want her to load up on summer school *and* Schooltastic! just to *make sure* that Shelby "gets ahead". Mr and Mrs Ruiz would never dream of comparing themselves to the kind of parents who make their little kid wear a bicycle helmet while playing soccer. Not only does the little kid look dorky, but you can't play soccer wearing a helmet! It would make your head feel like it weighed a thousand pounds. And I think that's how Shelby feels about what her parents expect of her – her head is heavy. Mr and Mrs Ruiz wouldn't see it but they are just like the parents of the little soccer player, wanting their kid to be so "safe" that they are actually *dragging them down*. I didn't think we'd made Shelby's load any lighter with our trip to Blue Cave either.

UP TO THE BLUFFS

Mid-Valley Road connects Surf Island Boulevard down in The Flats to Pine Barren Lane up in The

Bluffs. The whole road is probably only a mile long, but it snakes up the steep hill in a series of switch-backs so it seems longer. Once on Mid-Valley, Shelby was able to come out from under the blanket; her mom's real estate territory did not extend up into The Bluffs. We drove through the low-lying bank of fog that hangs over The Flats every morning and after-noon. On some days this fog never clears away – it just hangs over my neighbourhood like a soggy grey blanket. For some reason the weather up in The Bluffs is almost always sunny. Wyatt says it has a dif-ferent "microclimate". All I know is that in so many ways the top of the hill is nothing like the bottom of the hill. Yeah, sure, the houses are bigger, the lawns are like football fields, and the cars are all brand new and perpetually clean, but more than anything there was a completely different vibe in The Bluffs. Have you ever walked up to a five-on-five basketball game in the park and called "next"? You get ten guys glar-ing at you like, "Why are *you* here?" That's the main vibe of The Bluffs – it's as if all the smooth asphalt streets, tall angular hedges and scrolled wrought iron fences were standing guard and demanding to know, "Why are *you* here?" So I can't even imagine what the residents of The Bluffs thought when they saw a Dodge Ram pickup loaded down with seven wind-burned kids and a 243 pound Mastiff pull up in front of the biggest and most important estate of the family that *founded* the whole microclimate on top of the hill.

Ernie was a sales-rep for HydroBright, a water purification company. Apparently water has to be purified before you drink it. I don't exactly know how you clean water, but Ernie had a nice new HydroBright truck because *he* did. Ernie also must have had experience with driving up to huge estates, because when he pulled up in front of the fifteen foot black wrought iron gates of Falcon's Lair, he didn't hesitate to push a small button on a black box which I guessed was some type of intercom. I had never noticed it before because on the field trip, the gates had already been open.

"Can I help you?" a voice said from the box.

"These kids have some property to return to Mr Thorpe," Ernie said. It looked to me like Ernie would have preferred to be anywhere else but here.

"I'm afraid you'll have to make an appointment," the voice said.

"Hold up the box," Ernie said.

At first I didn't understand Ernie was speaking to

me. I must have looked really confused because Ernie sighed deeply as if to say, "Look what kind of idiots I'm stuck with."

"Hold up the box for the *camera*." Ernie pointed and indicated a sleek white rectangle with a lens poking out of it that was mounted high up on one of the gateposts. I looked over to Wyatt.

"Video surveillance," he said. "Show them the sextant."

So I stood up in the bed of the truck and opened the mahogany box to reveal the Golden Sextant. Suddenly, there was a buzzing sound and as if by magic the huge wrought iron gates started to glide open.

On the south end of Surf Island Boulevard there is a public park called Goat's Neck Park. It's pretty big – there's room for a playground and four soccer fields. I only mention this because it occurred to me that you could fit around 30 or 40 Goat's Neck Parks *on the front lawn* of Falcon's Lair. The back lawn is even *bigger*, and it connects with one of the fairways of The Bluffs Country Club, so you could say that Falcon's Lair is kind of in the middle of this enormous dark-green forest. Instead of the vibe being, "what are *you* doing here?" it was more like, "you absolutely *should not* be here." I guessed that my fellow Outriders were feeling the same way as we drove up the ultra-long drive to the estate. No one in the bed of the pickup said a word, they were just peering out at the groomed lawns and the really tall trees as if they were space aliens taking a look at earth for the first time.

"Mr Thorpe's going to think we stole it," Shelby whispered to me.

"Absolutely," I said.

FALCON'S LAIR

Ernie pulled the HydroBright truck around the circular drive towards the front doors of Falcon's Lair. Even though I had been to the mansion before, it looked even bigger and more imposing now that we weren't arriving with a hundred kids packed into a yellow school bus. There was this guy – who I imagined was a butler – waiting on the stone steps of the mansion. His expression didn't change when Ernie stopped the pickup right in front of the entrance.

The butler-guy either had really good manners or had already called the police – it was tough to tell. I looked up and saw a bunch more of the video surveillance cameras mounted at all the corners of the house. They were kind of hidden in the ivy, so I assumed there were a whole lot more that I couldn't see.

Before we all dismounted from the truck bed, Ernie called back to me from behind the wheel, "I can't hang out here. I gotta get back to work."

"That's OK; we'll walk home. Thanks for the lift," I said.

In the passenger seat, Viveca tilted her head slightly, her hair falling over her caramel-brown eyes. "Ernie, this was soooo sweet of you."

Ernie's cheeks flushed. A smile ripped across his face. Poor dude. He had no idea.

All of us had now gotten out of the back of the truck. Howie hopped down last and headed straight for a potted cypress just to the right of the entrance. The butler-guy took a step backwards, as Howie lumbered in his direction.

Ernie and Viveca peeled away in the HydroBright truck as Nar began to yell, "RAA! RAA!" I don't know much Thai, but I was very familiar with what "raa" meant. It meant "stop". But even though Nar considered himself a "dog whisperer" no man on earth could prevent Howie from heeding the call of nature. Howie lifted his right rear leg. Now the butler-guy's expression *did* change. It was the face of someone who had never before witnessed a 243 pound dog relieving himself. I'm not trying to be gross, but do the math. A Chihuahua lifts his leg, he does "a tinkle". When Howie lifts his leg, the only way to describe it is "a tidal wave". No question, the butler-guy was calculating the cost of replacing not just the pot the cypress tree was in, but the entire tree. Little did he know how fortunate he was that he didn't witness what we call the "Howie download". This wasn't the kind of grand heroic entrance I had pictured. I was just standing there holding the mahogany box, feeling really out of my element, when the butler-guy said, "Mr Thorpe is waiting for you in the solarium."

None of us moved. Perhaps it was because none of us knew what a "solarium" was. Luckily the butler-guy turned and headed into the front hallway of Falcon's Lair and not knowing what else to do, we all just sort of followed him – that is, all of us except Howie. Nar whispered something to him and Howie got comfortable at the bottom of the stone steps right in front of the mansion. One thing Howie could absolutely be counted on to do – he would stay right in that spot and not move even *one inch* until Nar returned.

Falcon's Lair is more like a museum than a place where someone actually lives. I couldn't identify one tenth of the stuff that was jammed into the rooms we passed. There were weird-looking sculptures, rugs hanging on the walls, and tons of paintings from the olden days. And when I say things were "jammed in", I mean it. The mansion was ultra-crowded. The seven of us had to walk single file through the centre hallway it was so *packed* with antiquities. We finally reached a glass-enclosed room at the back of the house which I deduced was the solarium because it was so sunny and all. There was a twelve-foot long model of a three-masted sailing schooner which I recognized from my field trip. It was a scale model of Commodore Sternmetz's schooner. This time I noticed the ship's name painted on the hull: *The Iris*. I was in the middle of wondering if Mr Thorpe had named his own sloop after Commodore Stermetz's ship when someone said, "Cam Walker! Greetings."

I froze in my tracks. So did the other Outriders. Standing in front of us was Mr Chapman Thorpe and, unless my brain was playing bizarre tricks with me, he had just called me by name – like he *knew* me.

I'm pretty cool under pressure. I can carve down the face of a ten-foot wave and never even consider the possibility of wiping out, but I have to admit, right at that moment I was sweating through my T-shirt. First of all I was confused: how was it possible that Mr Thorpe knew my name? Second of all: Mr Thorpe was kind of scary. He was over six feet tall but had to hunch over on these aluminum canes that he clutches in both hands. Maybe the name of the mansion, "Falcon's Lair", was in my head or something, but Mr Thorpe did give you the impression he was like some huge bird of prey. He had a really long thin nose and bright blue eyes that were really alert, like he could watch all seven of us at once. All I could manage to mumble was, "Um, how did . . ."

". . . I know your name?" It was like Mr Thorpe was *hearing* my thoughts. "I remember you, Cam, from your field trip. I overheard something you said and it stuck with me."

The rest of The Outriders looked like they had been frozen. The only detectable motion they made were small darting eye movements that ping-ponged back and forth between Mr Thorpe and me.

A bunch of thoughts raced through my brain but all I managed to say was, "Uhh?"

"You probably don't even remember, Cam, but you were staring at one of the 18th century tapestries in the ballroom and I heard you say, 'The world is full of a whole bunch of stuff I know nothing about.'" Mr Thorpe laughed at the memory of it. "I immediately asked one of the teachers who you were."

It sounded like something I might have said, but I couldn't remember saying it. I looked over at Shelby. She had no clue as to what was going on. Was Mr Thorpe trying to throw me off balance? Was he mocking me? Was he showing me that he knew exactly who I was and knew exactly where to find me if it became necessary? I should have asked him any one of these questions, but I said, "Oh."

"I feel exactly the same way!" Mr Thorpe must have registered that I wasn't following his train of thought. "I too feel the world is full of a whole bunch of stuff I know nothing about!" Mr Thorpe swept his hand towards all the antiquities in the room and said, "That's why I collect all of this. I'm trying to learn a few things."

Mr Thorpe smiled, at least I think it was a smile, but since he was a very old dude, when he curled the corners of his mouth upward, it showed a lot of the gums above his teeth and it looked more like a sneer. "Aren't you going to introduce me to your friends?"

While I introduced Shelby, Wyatt, Bettina, Din,

Nar and Ty it occurred to me that Mr Thorpe had not even ASKED about the Golden Sextant! What type of sick game was he playing? Was he stalling so the police or FBI could swoop in ninja-style and arrest us all for possession of stolen property? Can a twelve-year-old be sent to prison?

Again, as if my mind were broadcasting my thoughts directly into Mr Thorpe's brain, he said to me, "How did you come into possession of my Golden Sextant?"

There it was. At last we were getting to it. Before I could speak Shelby blurted out, "We didn't steal it!"

"Shelby, I didn't suspect you did." I noticed Mr Thorpe used Shelby's name when he addressed her. It must be some technique designed to creep people out so he could keep the upper hand.

"Jacques and Crystal. The sextant. Took." Wyatt was so unnerved he had lost control of the English language.

Mr Thorpe looked towards the butler-guy and said, "The trainers." He nodded, and the butler-guy went off somewhere – maybe to call the police or maybe to call in a hit squad of trained assassins to have Jacques and Crystal "erased".

"We saw them burying it at Blue Cave." I had

finally managed to speak a complete thought. I then handed the mahogany box to Mr Thorpe. He lifted the lid, gave the Golden Sextant a quick look and put the box down on a huge desk that was facing out towards the backyard rose garden. It looked like the desk was where Mr Thorpe did most of his sitting, no place else looked even remotely comfortable. I was amazed that Mr Thorpe didn't inspect the sextant more carefully. Maybe when you have so many billions of things, no one item is all that important. Mr Thorpe turned and looked right at me.

"Describe it to me," he said.

"The sextant?"

"Blue Cave! Were the plankton glowing?"

"Yeah. It was *awesome*."

"I sailed out there twenty-one years ago. I could get around much easier then. I'll never forget it." Mr Thorpe looked upward as if he was seeing a movie of his trip on a screen above his head.

"Neither will we," I said, just to keep the conversation going.

I saw Shelby steal a quick glance at her Swatch. Wyatt, Bettina, Din, Nar and Ty had all begun fidgeting slightly; they wanted to get out of this uncomfortable situation as much as I did.

"Um, Mr Thorpe?"

"Please, call me Chappy."

OK, that was never going to happen, but it was sort of weirdly cool that Mr Thorpe had said it. I said, "Um, we don't want to be rude or anything, but we have to be getting home."

"Not until I give all of you a reward."

I could feel all eyes of The Outriders on me as I said, "Um, no, sir."

"No reward?" Now Mr Thorpe looked confused. For some reason, that made me feel kind of good.

"We just wanted to give back the Golden Sextant. That's all."

Mr Thorpe's penetrating blue eyes scanned over the group of us. I don't think Mr Thorpe was a guy that was used to being surprised by people. It's like when we had walked into the room we were just some scruffy kids from down in The Flats and now he didn't know how to classify us. I would have felt amped to get a reward, but not as amped as I felt right now.

"At least let me get you some cookies and lemonade. You have a long hike down the hill on that hidden trail you use behind the golf course." And with that, Mr Thorpe kind of *clomped* out of the room leaving me wondering how I could have ever been insane enough to think I could get the upper hand with a guy like him.

"He knows about the Escape Trail," Nar whispered to me.

"He's freaky-scary," Bettina said.

"Absolutely," I said, just as Din's Bahtphone started ringing.

No one on earth had the number of the Bahtphone except The Outriders, and we were all standing in Mr Thorpe's solarium; so who could possibly be calling? Din hit the send button on the phone and lifted it to his ear. He looked confused, then handed the phone to Shelby. "It's for *you*," he said.

Shelby, who was equally confused, took the phone from Din just as the butler-guy re-entered the solarium and said, "Mr Thorpe would like you to join him for snacks in the breakfast nook."

Shelby was still on the phone. She looked oddly pale. She signalled for the rest of us to go ahead, and then held up one finger as if to say, "I'll just be a minute." The rest of us followed the butler-guy (hadn't gotten his name) single file back through all the antiquities in the main hallway into a huge room that was an offshoot of the even huger kitchen. I assumed this was the "breakfast nook" but it didn't have a "nook" feel to it. Mr Thorpe was standing near a twenty-foot dark wood table which was *piled* with cookies and lemonade. Some unseen cooks or servants had even put out cloth napkins, which none of us dared *touch* for fear of making them dirty. I saw Din and Nar eyeing the Matterhorn of cookies looming in front of them, and I made sure to shoot them a look. Even though Din and Nar are very small and wiry, they could eat their body weight in food, particularly if it contained sugar. Ty, who was ginormous, didn't need to eat *at all*, which none of us could figure out. Din and Nar understood the meaning of my look and they each carefully took *one* cookie, as did the rest of us.

Shelby came into the room a moment later and said, "Sorry. My parents called."

I knew for a fact she was lying, because her parents did NOT have the Bahtphone number and Shelby would have already been on her way to boarding school if her parents discovered she wasn't at Schooltastic! Something really strange was going on; I just didn't know what it was.

"I want to thank each and every one of you for

returning the sextant. I can't tell you how much it means to me." Mr Thorpe lifted a glass of lemonade, as if in a toast, and we all did the same.

"To The Outriders," Mr Thorpe said.

I guess we were supposed to repeat "To The Outriders," but we were all so massively, hugely, insanely freaked out that Mr Thorpe knew what we called ourselves that we all just stood there with our lemonades suspended in mid-air. Mr Thorpe's expression didn't betray his thoughts, but there was a little electric spark in his blue eyes that told me *he knew that we knew* we were fighting way above our weight class.

"I hope that we can all visit each other sometime very soon. I'll let Giorgio show you to the door. I'm due for my hydrotherapy."

The butler-guy (who I guess was named Giorgio) asked us if we wanted him to "arrange transportation". We politely declined and then he led us in a long serpentine out the front door and down the stone steps where Howie hadn't moved a millimetre. The moment Giorgio closed the front doors of Falcon's Lair, Shelby grabbed my arm.

"Jacques and Crystal kidnapped Annabelle," she said.

"Huh?" was all I could reply.

"They want the Golden Sextant. And we can't tell anyone or they're going to *hurt* Annabelle."

My head was spinning. "How'd they know Annabelle was your sister?"

"My mom was their estate agent! They had dinner in our dining room! They said they want to make the exchange at Sanctuary Bay in an hour."

Shelby unzipped her backpack to reveal that she had RESTOLEN THE GOLDEN SEXTANT. She had taken it out of the mahogany box; it was just stuffed into her backpack, gleaming like the fiery edges of the sun.

"But . . ." I didn't get the chance to finish my thought. Shelby grabbed my arm again.

"Come up with a plan. *Now*. We have to rescue my little sister."

CHAPTER EIGHT: SCAVENGING

This was the absolute, no-question, not-even-a-discussion, off-the-charts *hugest* and scariest thing that had ever happened to The Outriders. Sure, we'd had some injuries (Ty broke two fingers during a dirt-bike expedition); we'd had some close calls with security guards (Bettina was once forced to hide in a drainpipe for an entire day); and we'd had our share of parental intervention (our middle school principal had once issued a mass-detention); but we had *never, ever* been in a situation even close to a *KIDNAPPING*.

I have to admit it – I was scared. Not the I'm-going-to-get-caught-scavenging-a-golf-cart kind of scared. This kind of fear was new to me. I actually felt like someone had gut-punched me just below the ribs; like there wasn't enough oxygen to fill my lungs. I found myself opening my mouth to breathe. The others didn't notice because we were now descending from The Bluffs which entailed rushing down the Escape Trail – pretty arduous even *without* all the additional stress. Also, I didn't *want* anyone to see me afraid because they were all depending on me to come up with a plan. If they saw I was losing it, *they* would lose it and we could be of no help to Annabelle. I once read an article in *Surfer Magazine* about this dude who rode the big waves on the North Shore of Oahu. He said that only an insane or deceased person didn't have fear of a thirty-foot wave. He said that he tried to "use his fear" to make him more alert and more in tune with the force of the ocean. So that's what I decided to do – use my fear as a weapon to attack this HUGE PROBLEM of how to rescue Annabelle.

I knew one thing for certain – we had to call the police or the FBI or even our parents. But Jacques and Crystal had said they would hurt Annabelle if we told *anyone*. And if they were willing to steal the most valuable object in our town right out from under the nose of one of the wealthiest men in the state, they were clearly capable of anything. So there was no alternative; *we* had to rescue Annabelle without any help from anyone and we had to figure out a way to do it in less than an hour.

Shelby had been leading our group down the Escape Trail. She was the most limber and quickest of anyone, so the rest of us had to work ultra-hard to keep up with her weaving around the boulders and through the underbrush. Howie lagged far behind, not feeling any of the urgency the rest of us did.

Shelby must have been getting impatient with the time it was taking for me to formulate a plan because all of a sudden she stopped, turned to me and said, "So?"

I don't know why, but in that very moment I realized two *hugely important* things.

THE FIRST HUGELY IMPORTANT THING I REALIZED:

Even though the kidnapping of her sister was the worst thing that could have ever happened to Shelby, she had completely stopped thinking about summer school or Schooltastic! – she was only thinking about the new expedition to rescue Annabelle. The spark had returned to Shelby's eyes – and she was back leading all of The Outriders down the Escape Trail! So the hugely important thing was that even though Shelby had every reason to be scared, worried or really angry – she was calm, focused and the first one charging into battle – she was back to being the same Shelby we all remembered!

THE SECOND HUGELY IMPORTANT THING I REALIZED:

I had a plan and I thought it could work.

But before I could lay it all out, the Bahtphone rang. This time it wasn't a normal ring tone, it was more of a *ping-ping* sound. I looked a Din.

"Text?"

Din shook his head. "Pix." Din pushed a series of buttons on the Bahtphone. We all crowded around to get a look.

On the tiny screen of the PDA we saw a video image of Annabelle sitting on a chair. She didn't look hurt or scared or dishevelled, she looked pretty much the same as she did at any other time. She sat calmly with her hands in the lap of her "uniform", looking directly at what must have been a cell phone camera. We then heard a male voice (must have been Jacques) say, "Go ahead."

But Annabelle just sat there. She didn't move a

muscle. She didn't smile, she didn't cower; she just *stared*.

Then we heard a female voice (Crystal) shout, "Say it, girly!"

Again, Annabelle said *nothing*. Suddenly, two female legs (Crystal again) entered the picture and walked directly towards Annabelle. The female figure, who had a distinctive hammerhead shark tattooed on her lower back (the camera angle didn't show Crystal's face) crossed towards the six-year-old and then "plinged" Annabelle on the side of the cheek.

"You tell them, girly! Tell them not to be going to the police!"

I guess Crystal thought Annabelle would find this "plinging" gesture threatening and it would kind of *force* Annabelle to speak. But Annabelle's expression didn't change. She didn't utter a single word. What she *did* do was bite down on Crystal's finger. Hard.

We heard Crystal scream, "OWWWWWWW!" Then the video clip ended.

Nar looked up from the Bahtphone. "Annabelle rocks," he said.

Jacques and Crystal Requin were now learning what countless babysitters at the Ruiz home had come to understand – Annabelle was so dangerous she was almost radioactive. But the Bahtphone message also made us all focus on how real this situation was.

Shelby turned to me. "You got a plan?"

"I do," I said, "but we need gear. A lot of gear."

"So let's go get it," Shelby said, and started back down the hill.

GETTING THE GEAR

Most of the stuff was readily accessible. Some of it was easy to scavenge, some we actually owned. But there was one item on the list, the mother-of-all-gear, which was going to be extremely tricky to get our hands on. Actually it was more than extremely tricky – it was close to impossible.

At the base of the Escape Trail I turned to Wyatt and said, "The time has come."

Wyatt knew exactly what this meant but wasn't thrilled about it.

"It's for Shelby and Annabelle." The favour I was asking Wyatt was so ginormous; I felt like he needed to be reminded about what was at stake.

"Just try to protect me on this," Wyatt said.

"I'll do my best."

Wyatt reached into his backpack and pulled out a

small key attached to a miniature replica of a buoy. This was a duplicate key to the Yamaha WaveRunner GP 1300 – also known as the mother-of-all-gear. I don't know if you're familiar with personal watercraft, but the Yamaha WaveRunner GP 1300 was like the big Kahuna of all personal watercraft. Picture sitting on top of a jet engine bolted to a razor-sharp fibre-glass hull; and then imagine rocketing across the waves at over 60 miles per hour. Then try to envision the Yamaha WaveRunner GP 1300 *passing you* as if you were standing still.

There was not one but *two* matching Yamaha WaveRunner GP 1300s three hundred yards from where we were standing alongside Surf Island Boulevard. They were moored at Surf Island Salvage which was the business owned by Morgan and Betty Kolbacher, Wyatt's mom and dad. Right about now you might be wondering, "If the Yamaha is so important to the expedition, why doesn't Wyatt just ask his mom and dad to borrow it?" Obviously you don't know Morgan and Betty Kolbacher.

Morgan Kolbacher (Chief Petty Officer, U.S. Navy, Ret.) runs Surf Island Salvage, and Betty Kolbacher runs Morgan. Morgan is fond of saying, "For twenty-five years I reported to the U.S. Navy and I'm pretty sure the U.S. Navy reported to Betty." Morgan is like six-foot-six, and Betty's just a little over five foot so Betty must have a bunch of skills we in The Outriders don't understand. All things being equal, I would have *liked* to have Morgan and Betty help us with our huge problem. But even though Morgan had retired from the Navy, he did everything "by the book" and would have immediately called the police or the Coast Guard to help rescue Annabelle. So instead of going *through* the Kolbachers we had to go *around* them.

If you looked at Sternmetz Marina from the air, it would look like a plastic pocket comb. Jutting out from a rickety old boardwalk there are a series of small docks that would look like the teeth of the pocket comb. At the very end of the comb, where you find that last thick tooth that is bigger than all the skinny ones in the middle; that would be the location of Surf Island Salvage.

From sun-up to sundown you can find Morgan and Betty in the nerve centre of Surf Island Salvage, which is a low, square, weatherworn wooden shack that has windows on all four sides. From this vantage point Morgan and Betty can keep a constant vigil over the mountains of rusted anchors, barnacle-encrusted buoys, and assorted keels, tillers, pulleys, cleats, shackles, forestays, propellers, sparkplugs, and algae-coated winches that used to be part of local sea vessels. Morgan's ancient grey steel desk, which had originally been in a map room of a World War II destroyer, was butted directly up to the window facing east, because this provided the clearest and most direct view of Mr and Mrs Kolbacher's most precious possessions – the twin purple Yamaha WaveRunner GP 1300s.

I need to make something clear – Mr and Mrs Kolbacher weren't mean or evil or anything. They were just two people who loved their watercraft and had ABSOLUTELY FORBIDDEN Wyatt from ever "scavenging" the Yamahas. There were several very solid reasons for this:

1. The Kolbachers' weren't in any way rich. The Cedar Cape Bank was the real owner of the Yamahas.
2. The Kolbachers' insurance didn't cover any "operators" other than Morgan and Betty.
3. The WaveRunners were essentially *racing* watercraft (GP stood for Grand Prix) and way too much machine for 12-year-old Wyatt to handle safely.

But nevertheless, if we were going to rescue Annabelle we *had* to scavenge one of the Yamahas. We also needed to try to conceal Wyatt's involvement in our plan. His dad, Morgan, stayed very calm most of the time. Not many people choose to bother a six-foot-six ex-Navy guy with bulging Popeye-like forearms burnished with mermaid tattoos. Betty was another story. Her temper was like a tea-kettle that was kept on a medium flame – it just needed a tiny bit of heat to boil over. And the thing that made her angriest were boaters who did not observe the speed markers inside the Marina buoys and kicked up wakes that rocked the Yamahas and caused them to bump against each other or the tyres that were festooned on the pier pilings. So if Wyatt was going to continue living in the Kolbacher family, we had to successfully scavenge one of the WaveRunners and make it look like Wyatt had absolutely nothing to do with it. I actually had that part figured out pretty well. Morgan and Betty weren't the hardest obstacle facing this operation – Sabre was.

Sabre was directly above me suspiciously sniffing between the planks of the pier, sensing my presence. I was in my wet suit, hugging one of the thick wooden pilings so I could hide in the shadows underneath the salvage pier. The water in the Marina was dark brown and had a shiny layer of gasoline that floated along the surface. I could feel crabs scuffling over my ankles just above my snorkelling flippers. My current situation was just about as far as you could get from the glowing beauty of Blue Cave. The Kolbachers claim that their dog Sabre is a "Doberman mix". It was fairly easy to see the Doberman part of Sabre – he had a thin pointy face and sharp triangular ears that were always pitched high in the "radar position". The biggest question we all had about Sabre was what the Doberman was "mixed" with. The dog had a powerful barrel-chested body and a tail that curved up and around like a roller-coaster loop. Bettina had seen a picture of a Japanese dog called an Akita which kind of had a body and tail like Sabre. The only reason we spent time wondering what two dogs could have possibly combined to create Sabre was that they must have been the meanest, angriest, most bloodthirsty dogs on earth. Sabre hated every living thing except Morgan, Betty and Wyatt. In reality, he *tolerated* Morgan and Wyatt and only really had affection for Betty. Sabre even hated *non-living* things and we would often see him bite into a hank of rope and tear it to shreds for absolutely no reason at all. During

Sabre's years on earth, not even one rusty bolt has been stolen from Surf Island Salvage.

To make matters worse, Sabre makes his bed on top of a tangled web of old hemp fishing nets that sits under the eaves of the Salvage company office right below the east facing window. This way Sabre can keep his malevolent yellow eyes trained on the twin purple Yamahas. *Now* you know why I was concealing myself under the pier and why we desperately needed a major distraction.

"Hey, Swabby!" For some reason "Swabby" was the nickname that Mr Kolbacher had for Wyatt. It might have something to do with the Navy, but I don't know much about the Navy.

Wyatt's arrival at the salvage yard signalled that the operation was underway. I couldn't see much from underneath the pier, just flickers of dark and light as Wyatt, Morgan, Betty and Sabre moved around on top of the pier's planks.

"Hiya, Dad," Wyatt said as he headed for the door of the office.

"How was Blue Cave?" Betty asked Wyatt.

"Cool," Wyatt said kind of casually, as if he wasn't involved in the biggest and most dangerous expedition of his life.

"There's string cheese if you're hungry." Betty always had a healthy supply of string cheese available even though Wyatt had stopped eating it around the age of five.

"Cool." Wyatt was really playing up the "casualness".

Suddenly I heard the mallard call. Immediately Sabre emitted a low husky growl. Even though I couldn't *see* what was happening, I *knew* what had drawn the attention of the dog. Sabre had heard two sounds coming from the boardwalk-end of the pier. The first sound was the horrific-sounding mallard call, and the second was a paper bag full of fresh anchovy fishing bait being tossed over the chain link fence surrounding the salvage yard. I could hear the scraping of Sabre's toenails on the wooden planks above me as he raced towards the location of the noise.

There's one more important thing you need to know about Sabre. Deep within his tiny evil brain, he has reserved a special ultra-vicious hate for one particular species of animal – the seagull. And here's an important thing you need to know about seagulls – they go INSANE for anchovies. If you've ever been fishing off a dock and used cut-up anchovies for bait, it is very possible that you have hooked a seagull by mistake because a gull will snatch an anchovy right out of mid-air while you are casting your line! Usually seagulls are smart, they can survive almost anywhere and can fly thousands of miles. But they lose any type of intelligence they have when they get a whiff of anchovy. And now, even though there was a vicious seagull-hating-Doberman-mix-hound-from-hell baring his teeth below them, a squadron of seagulls started to dive bomb the pier, trying to pick off pieces of ambrosial anchovies.

Shelby was the one who had tossed the bait into the salvage yard. She was hiding outside the perimeter of the chain link fence behind an enormous spool of metal cable (the same cable we had scavenged for the zip line). Normally Sabre would have sensed her presence but by this time he had gone totally BERSERK trying to catch and rip apart a seagull. Before you think we Outriders are totally cruel, I'll tell you something else you need to know about seagulls. They are wicked-good at not getting caught by dogs. They seem to know when to dive and when to retreat and manage to stay ahead of even the most cunning of canines. Actually, this flock of gulls seemed to *enjoy* driving Sabre mad. Sabre wasn't sophisticated in his rage. He snapped at every seagull he saw, never pursuing any one seagull for very long. Also, his fury was very predictable – he only lunged for the bird that was right in front of him. So pretty quickly the seagulls figured out a system. One bird would swoop in front of Sabre while fifteen other birds picked off the anchovies *behind* him. I don't know exactly how you measure decibels but the sound that Sabre made would have been off the loudness chart which is why the dog made the best distraction in the world.

I heard Morgan and Betty running down to the far end of the pier. I imagined they were waving their arms frantically trying to "shoo" the seagulls away from Sabre. That's when I made my move. I slipped deeper into the water and snaked my way along the pier pilings till I was directly behind the purple Yamahas. I silently slipped the mooring rope from the rusty cleat that tethered one of the WaveRunners to the pier. I had Wyatt's duplicate key but couldn't risk starting the Yamaha for fear of alerting Morgan and Betty. So I gently pushed the watercraft out away from the pier and slowly guided it towards the next "tooth" of the Marina "comb" where there were a bunch of old Boston Whaler bass boats moored to a pier. I felt someone swim up alongside me and knew it was Shelby. She had a blue waterproof duffle-bag looped around her shoulder. I knew the Golden Sextant was inside it. As per our plan, she had thrown a second bag of anchovies into the salvage yard and then slipped into the water to help me with the Yamaha. Just as we managed to guide the watercraft to the far side of one of the bass boats, I turned back towards the salvage yard. I watched as Wyatt raced out of the salvage office holding an air horn. He raced towards his mom and dad then *blasted* the air horn which emitted an earsplitting klaxon SHRIEK. This horrible noise didn't affect Sabre at all, he still snapped and growled with murderous rage, but it did bother the seagulls, and they dispersed, having picked up every last bit of anchovy before flying off. Of course the deafening blast of the air horn also concealed the high-octane growl of the Yamaha WaveRunner GP 1300 as I turned the key in the ignition. Shelby climbed onto the purple seat behind me and we slowly glided out of the Marina, careful to keep ourselves screened from the salvage yard, hiding the Yamaha behind much larger and slower vessels. We both looked over our shoulders towards Surf Island Salvage. Morgan and Betty were patting Wyatt on the shoulder, congratulating him for having the presence of mind to "save the day" and scare the seagulls away with the air horn. Behind his back, Wyatt was giving us the thumbs up sign, wishing us luck in rescuing Annabelle.

CHAPTER NINE: EXCHANGING

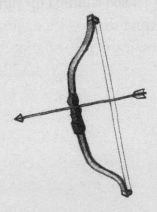

Sanctuary Bay sounds like it would be a beautiful spot, but it's not. You might think it's part of a wildlife preserve, but it isn't. You may wonder if the high rock formations that define its boundaries give the tiny bay a church-like feel, but they don't. The reality is that Sanctuary Bay is an ugly V-shaped gouge in the coastline that has only one positive attribute – it is very secluded and therefore an excellent place for two kidnappers to exchange a six-year-old girl for a Golden Sextant and not worry about being spotted.

I had to give Jacques and Crystal credit. They had chosen a spot that gave them almost all the tactical advantages for the exchange. I say "almost" because there were a few things about Sanctuary Bay that I was sure Jacques and Crystal *didn't* know. They hadn't grown up in Surf Island so unless they had extensively explored every inch of the coast they probably wouldn't have known about the run-off pipe.

We had discovered the pipe by accident during an earlier expedition; we had scavenged some sailboards and a strong wind had blown us off course. We ended up beaching ourselves on the tiny strip of sand inside of Sanctuary Bay. When we saw the six foot wide run-off pipe we were naturally curious as to where it led. When we got back to town we dug out the map of the city water system that Ty's dad, Mr Dyminczyk, had in his Town of Surf Island Water Department truck. We discovered that the run-off pipe was part of a huge underground rain drainage system. It actually was possible for us to enter a manhole right in the centre of Surf Island Boulevard and *walk underground* all the way to Sanctuary Bay (unless it was raining and the pipes were flooded with water). This was such a cool thing to do we made the subterranean trip dozens of times. Which is why we knew so much about Sanctuary Bay and why Ty, Din, Nar and Howie were somewhere deep underground heading towards the mouth of the pipe at that very moment.

I was certain of their location because it was all part of THE PLAN. I'm not bragging, but the strategy I had devised was really excellent. The underlying foundation of the plan was the basic fact that as long as we retained control of the Golden Sextant we had the upper hand. Yes, Jacques and Crystal had Annabelle and she obviously was more valuable *to us*, but the sextant was the only thing of value *to them*. Simple logic dictated that it was in Jacques and Crystal's best interest to deliver Annabelle in good shape because if they didn't they'd risk not getting the sextant and a whole host of other trouble they wanted no part of (police, FBI, Interpol). However, once we gave up control of the sextant it was impossible to guess what would happen. We didn't know Jacques and Crystal well enough to predict if they were the type of criminals who wanted to make sure that there were no witnesses to their crimes. So, in success, the best results of the plan would be to:

1. Rescue Annabelle.
2. Not give up the Golden Sextant.

3. Make sure Jacques and Crystal were brought to justice.
4. Return the Golden Sextant to Mr Thorpe.
5. Have no one find out what happened.
6. Make it back to Schooltastic! by 7 o'clock.

I know, our goals seemed ambitious, but I had read this article in *Surfer Magazine* about this guy who coached pro surfers and advised all his athletes to "strive for perfection and accept excellence". It is possible I was just a bit cocky; my plan was *that* good. The best part about it – it didn't rely on luck.

THE PLAN TO RESCUE ANNABELLE

Shelby and I were cruising along, riding atop the powerful Yamaha WaveRunner, a few hundred yards to the north of Sanctuary Bay, when we heard Bettina's voice over our walkie-talkie.

"I'm in position."

"Copy that." Even though Wyatt couldn't be with us for this part of the operation, I felt I had to honour him by using the "walkie-speak".

Although Shelby and I couldn't see her, we knew that Bettina was hiding in a craggy rock formation about seventy-five feet above the tiny beach that was tucked deep into the "V" of Sanctuary Bay. We also knew she had two crucial pieces of gear – a length of mountain-climbing rope and her bow and arrows.

Shelby and I then heard a click of static from the walkie-talkie which was Ty signalling that he, Din, Nar and Howie were in place concealed in the run-off pipe a few dozen yards from the mouth.

"Intel?" I said to Bettina, knowing she had a clear view of the bay from her post atop the cliffs.

"Just like you drew it up," she radioed back.

I have to admit, I felt pretty good about myself. Bettina's last transmission confirmed that my prediction about how Jacques and Crystal would handle the exchange was a hundred per cent accurate. Jacques would be waiting for us on the beach of Sanctuary Bay. Crystal and Annabelle would be in a boat south of the bay waiting for a signal from Jacques that we had kept up our end of the bargain (brought the Golden Sextant and didn't notify the police). Since Jacques and Crystal didn't have a big sophisticated network of co-conspirators, there was almost no other way for them to manage the exchange of the sextant for Annabelle.

I also knew that Jacques and Crystal's plan relied on one major assumption – that they were dealing with "kids" and therefore *they* had the upper hand.

THE TWO HUGEST MISTAKES PEOPLE MAKE:

1. Kids underestimating the intelligence of adults.
2. Adults underestimating the intelligence of kids.

Jacques and Crystal were counting on us to have this go down the way *they* wanted it to. Our job was to make sure it didn't go that way. I knew that as soon as Shelby and I cruised into the bay without a police escort Jacques would demand to see the Golden Sextant. Then he was going to order us to *give* him the sextant. He'd then expect us to demand to see Annabelle, and he'd radio for Crystal to pull her boat into the bay so we could see that Annabelle hadn't been mistreated (other than being kidnapped). Then he would be expecting us to hand over the Golden Sextant. If we did what they asked we would be handing them ALL OF THE CONTROL. They might release Annabelle, or they might not. One smart option would be to take along Annabelle as "insurance" until they felt they were far enough away that they couldn't be pursued or caught. Their plan had one very serious flaw – Jacques and Crystal were only *two people*. At some point Crystal, who was in the boat, had to pick up Jacques, who was on the beach. It was at that moment that *my* plan would take over and *their* plan would unravel.

Before Shelby and I pulled into the north side of the bay, she stowed the waterproof duffle containing the Golden Sextant in the cargo compartment of the WaveRunner. On the run from the Marina I had discovered that the Yamaha was so enormously powerful that even the slightest twist of my wrist on the throttle caused the watercraft to *lunge* forward and kick up a rooster tail of sea spray behind us. So I was careful to just *nudge* the throttle so that Shelby and I entered the bay as *slowly* as possible. I was hoping to give the impression that we were just two scared kids in a situation that was way over our heads. Also, our slow speed would allow Jacques and Crystal time to realize we hadn't brought along any of the authorities.

One thing that was important – Shelby and I had to stay *on the water*; if we made the mistake of getting off the Yamaha we would lose our tactical advantage.

As soon as I got about thirty yards offshore, I took my hand off the throttle and let the Yamaha idle.

"Did you bring it, the sextant?" Jacques yelled from the beach in his Belgian-ish accent.

"We did," I said.

Shelby stood on the side rails of the Yamaha, opened the storage compartment, and pulled out the blue waterproof duffle. She then unzipped it, revealing the gleaming gold of the sextant.

"Let me have it."

Shelby and I had talked over ever single move we would make. Without me saying a word, Shelby zipped the sextant back into the blue duffle and stowed it in the storage compartment.

"Show me Annabelle first!" I yelled to Jacques.

Jacques picked up a walkie-talkie and said something into it. Seconds later, Shelby and I heard the deep roar of an outboard engine and Crystal pulled into the south side of the bay, piloting a Bayliner waterskiing boat with a 125 horsepower outboard Mercury at the stern. We could see the petite figure of Annabelle seated calmly in one of the rear seats, her school "uniform" still perfectly clean and pressed. Crystal had a big bandage wrapped around the finger that Annabelle had bitten. Her index finger jutted straight out as if she was perpetually signalling "just one minute". Bad finger and all, Crystal managed to navigate the Bayliner to a stop fifteen yards offshore and became the third point of a triangle formed also by Shelby and me on our Yamaha and Jacques standing on the beach.

"Throw me it, the sextant, and I will let you have her, the girl!" Jacques yelled.

Shelby stood on the side rails and opened the storage compartment of the purple Yamaha. She pulled out the blue duffle. I knew that Jacques would expect me to say something before handing over the sextant, so I said it.

"Let Annabelle go and I'll give you the sextant!"

Jacques laughed. This was going just as he had expected.

"You don't want to see her hurt, the little girl. Let's get over with this."

I nodded to Shelby. She reared back and *threw* the blue duffle. But she threw it towards CRYSTAL in the waterskiing boat! The Golden Sextant bobbed on the surface for a moment or two and slowly began to sink.

"YOU IDIOTS!" Jacques yelled from the beach.

Instantly, Crystal dived into the bay in order to

rescue the sextant before it sank to the bottom.

Jacques and Crystal had no way of knowing that Shelby's "bad throw" was completely intentional. But they might have gotten an inkling that things weren't going their way when Ty, Nar, Din and Howie appeared at the mouth of the run-off pipe and Din yelled, "ANNABELLE!"

Jacques spun around and froze. He was really caught off guard seeing two small boys, one hulking tall boy and a 243 pound Mastiff staring at him from the run-off drain.

One thing you can absolutely say about Annabelle is that she is not stupid. She immediately understood this was her opportunity to escape and she took it. With the speed of a lightning bolt, she dived into the water and started paddling for shore.

Nar shouted an urgent command to Howie. "*Pajon!*" This was Thai for "attack!"

At this very moment Bettina had rappelled midway down the face of the cliff and was launching flaming arrows towards Crystal's now empty water-skiing boat in order to set it afire and disable it.

Annabelle reached the beach and started a mad sprint for the run-off pipe where Ty, Din and Nar were waiting for her. They would spirit her away into the recesses of the pipe while Howie subdued Jacques, and Bettina destroyed the only means that the kidnappers would have to pursue us. At least that was what was *supposed to happen*. None of it did.

Howie kind of messed everything up. Even though Nar was screaming, "*PA-JON! PA-JON!*" over and over again, Howie didn't charge. He never even moved. He just stood there in the mouth of the run-off pipe. I was even suspicious that Howie didn't know what "*Pa-jon*" meant.

Jacques might have been surprised by the sneak attack, but only for a moment. Before Annabelle could reach the safety of the run-off pipe, Jacques lifted her into the air, making sure to wrap his massive arms around her so she would be unable to kick, bite, scratch or claw.

Meanwhile Bettina's flaming arrows had hit their mark, each of them landing in the waterskiing boat. We all had hoped for a fiery-orange ball of explosion, but instead, as each of the arrows hit the fibreglass hull with a dull "thwink" sound, the flame extinguished. No flames. No fiery-orange explosions.

By this time Crystal had managed to rescue the blue duffle bag and open it. She had discovered that

Shelby and I still had the Golden Sextant in the storage compartment of our Yamaha.

"Those brats switched it!" Crystal yelled as she climbed back into the waterskiing boat. By this time Bettina was out of arrows and the fire raining out of the sky had stopped.

Jacques had Annabelle tightly squeezed in the python grip of his arms. He now looked more amused than surprised. He sneered at Howie and then said, "Stupid dog."

Click. That switch deep within Nar's brain flipped to "on". It was "bpai" time and Nar charged out of the mouth of the pipe, his face contorted in rage. Jacques had insulted Howie and this, combined with the fact that Howie had not responded to his master's command, turned Nar into a compact ball of pure fury. In a millisecond, Nar had leaped onto Jacques' back and was punching, kicking and biting the Belgian. This lasted for all of two seconds, as Jacques shrugged his massive shoulders and back, flinging Nar a full ten feet, sending him sprawling into the surf. Jacques didn't realize it at that moment, but he had just triggered a sequence of events that would lead to his doom.

As much as Nar loved Howie, that was how Howie

felt about Nar. You could set off a stick of dynamite next to Howie and he would barely even change his "comfortable" position. But if you laid a hand on Nar, you could be sure that a 243 pound locomotive with teeth was headed your way. Jacques was fortunate that he saw Howie coming. Howie, normally one of the slowest moving animals on earth, needed only three strides before he POUNCED like some kind of freakishly-enormous panther. Jacques only had time to act reflexively. He tossed Annabelle aside like some type of Raggedy Ann doll and did the only thing any living being would do in a similar situation – *he ducked and covered his head with his hands*. Howie absolutely FLATTENED Jacques. There was a sound like a beach ball exploding, which was the sound of all the air rushing out of Jacques' lungs.

Immediately, Din and Ty took Annabelle by the hand.

"Took you idiots long enough," was all she said.

Then Din and Ty helped Nar to his feet and RACED back into the inky blackness of the run-off pipe. Howie, who was now standing on Jacques' back and GROWLING (and also drooling), swivelled his head and looked back towards the run-off pipe. Sensing that Nar was out of danger, Howie's ferociousness just simply disappeared and he casually hopped off of Jacques' back and loped back into the run-off pipe and disappeared.

Jacques got to his feet slowly, realizing he had just been given a second chance to walk the face of the earth. For a moment he started towards the run-off pipe, but only a true moron would rush into a darkened tunnel with no flashlight knowing there was a dog the size of Howie ahead of him.

"FORGET THE KID! WE GOTTA GET THE SEXTANT!" Crystal screamed as she pushed the throttle and charged the Bayliner towards the shore to pick up Jacques.

I didn't waste any time, I rolled my wrist heavily on the Yamaha's throttle and Shelby and I blasted out of the mouth of the bay into the open ocean.

ONE OF THE DIFFERENCES BETWEEN MOVIES AND REAL LIFE: In the movies, Tom Cruise would have been piloting the Yamaha WaveRunner GP 1300. In real life, it was me. In the movies, Tom would have been a world-champion-level watercraft pilot. In real life, I gave the Yamaha's throttle such a huge twist that Shelby and I almost immediately became AIRBORNE. That sounds like a good thing, but it's not, because the

WaveRunner, or any watercraft for that matter, needs to be *in the water* to gain speed. Being in the air actually *slows you down*. Even though the Bayliner was heavier, Crystal managed to keep its 125-horsepower outboard *in the water*, and she and Jacques were ROCKETING right towards us!

It wasn't hard to figure out the intentions of Jacques and Crystal. They were angry – really, really angry – and wanted to vent their frustrations by *ramming* us. Yes, they wanted to take back the Golden Sextant, but we had embarrassed them so they also wanted to hurt us.

HERE WERE OUR OPTIONS:

1. Run.

It would have been so much better if Tom Cruise had been piloting the Yamaha, but he was nowhere in sight. Remember that discussion about Howie, the dinghy and ballast? Well, we could have used a whole lot more ballast. The Yamaha kept wanting to leave the water and take flight and I wasn't experienced enough to know how to keep it in the water.

We had about five seconds before the waterskiing boat's hull would smash us to pieces.

"LEAN – LIKE THE KAYAK!" Shelby screamed over the roar of the engine. Shelby yanked my shoulders to one side forcing the Yamaha to tilt and suddenly it was as if the WaveRunner gained traction and Shelby and I were slingshotted across the waves. I didn't dare look back but I could imagine the surprise on Jacques and Crystal's faces when they fell fifty yards behind in the blink of an eye.

The problem with the whole *leaning* technique was that it caused us to *turn*. I knew exactly how to compensate for this on a kayak when you are going about two miles per hour, but at 65 miles per hour every little decision you make is amplified to the max. So while I was trying to learn how to become a Tom Cruise-level WaveRunner pilot, we were making huge zigzags across the ocean. The Yamaha was kicking up a massive hurricane of sea foam which was spraying back towards Jacques and Crystal, dousing them with mist. This slowed them down just a little which was good because their boat was *really fast* and was able to keep up with the Yamaha. I looked down at the gas gauge; I had plenty of fuel, but absolutely no plan.

As if listening to my thoughts, Shelby yelled, "HEAD FOR GOAT'S NECK!"

I didn't have any time to think about this as Shelby yanked my shoulders to the right, sending us in the direction she thought we should go. If I did have time to think about it, I would have concluded that her idea was a good one. Goat's Neck was that skinny strip of land that connected the town of Surf Island to the rest of the coast. But the reason Shelby's plan was smart was that Goat's Neck is surrounded by marshes and narrow channels. Some of the channels cut through the marsh, some of the channels are dead ends. Shelby and I knew that area well; there wasn't a chance that Jacques and Crystal did.

ANOTHER DIFFERENCE BETWEEN MOVIES AND REAL LIFE:

In the movies Tom Cruise would zoom into the narrow channels, expertly manoeuvre his Yamaha WaveRunner GP 1300 through the cattails and then make one awesome world-champion hairpin turn into the tiniest, most narrow channel that *only he knew about* and the bad guys in the boat that was pursuing him would *miss the turn* and ram into a supertanker that just happened to be docked on the other side of the marsh. In real life, I zoomed into the narrow channel *way too fast* and the Yamaha rammed into a thicket of marsh reeds. Luckily, Shelby and I sort of plowed over the reeds and the Yamaha acted like a kind of nautical lawnmower chewing up the tall green stalks and spitting them out. This sounds kind of Tom Cruise-like and cool but it wasn't because we *lost a lot of speed* and Jacques and Crystal were barrelling down on us. If I could have made a hairpin turn into a super-narrow channel that only I knew about, I would have. But instead, I plowed along the widest channel I could, just praying I wouldn't hit any submerged stumps or sandbars.

It was insanely easy for the waterskiing boat to navigate the channel for the simple reason that they could clearly see that our Yamaha hadn't run aground, so since they weren't drawing much water, they could pretty much go where we went. And the amazing thing about travelling this fast across the water is that you cover a lot of distance *really quickly* and before we knew it, we had blasted out of the marsh and were headed right towards the town directly south of Surf Island – Cedar Cape.

"CEDAR CAPE!" Shelby yelled, and I knew exactly what she meant.

Without any coaxing from Shelby, I leaned to the

right and the Yamaha shot forward, heading directly for the town of Cedar Cape and more importantly towards the one location that every single resident of Cedar Cape was most proud of – THE CEDAR CAPE COAST GUARD STATION.

We were so digging on ourselves for finding a safe harbour that we didn't notice Jacques and Crystal had closed the gap between us and Jacques was leaping from the bow of his boat onto our Yamaha!

Jacques latched his powerful hands onto Shelby's shoulders, and for a moment became a third passenger on the purple WaveRunner. But once again he had underestimated Shelby simply because she was a kid, and Shelby used Jacques' own strength against him; she Aikido-flipped him off of her back and sent him crashing into the water. At this speed Jacques' body became like a skipping stone and he bounced a couple of times before splashing into the ocean. Crystal expertly made a hairpin turn and pulled back on the throttle, then helped Jacques out of the water. This delay gave Shelby and me time to power right between the harbour buoys and blast towards the Coast Guard Station. The whole chase would have ended right there except for one thing – the Coasties were out on a call!

The forty-four-foot motor lifeboat that was usually docked at the station wasn't there! Suddenly I heard the roar of the 125 horsepower Mercury outboard and turned to see Jacques and Crystal building up ramming speed. We had made a fatal error – Shelby and I were now trapped in the confines of the crescent-shaped harbour with no wiggle room to escape. Only one thing prevented us from having the Bayliner smash us into the watery abyss – a purple Yamaha WaveRunner GP 1300 travelling 65 miles per hour appeared from out of nowhere and cut across Jacques and Crystal's bow! Wyatt could never stand to be left out, especially if we were on an expedition.

In order to avoid being rammed by Wyatt, Crystal yanked the steering wheel of the Bayliner. But she yanked too hard. The Mercury outboard was so insanely powerful that it lifted the rear of the water-skiing boat out of the water and caused it to FLIP, kind of in slow motion, like a football doing a lazy spiral. Luckily for Jacques and Crystal they were thrown far from the boat. They both splashed into the water. Their Bayliner hit the water upside down; a second or two later the Mercury engine snapped off the transom and promptly sunk out of sight. A second or two after that, Jacques and Crystal surfaced, angry beyond words but unhurt. And finally, a second or two after *that* a shadow crossed over Jacques' and Crystal's faces. They looked up to see the Coast Guard forty-four-foot motor lifeboat *Providence* dropping anchor right beside them.

Wyatt, Shelby and I didn't even take a nano-second to enjoy the moment of our conquest. Without any communication between the two Yamahas, we both turned north and rocketed back towards Surf Island. It was 6:30. If we went full throttle, Shelby could be back to Schooltastic! before 7 P.M. and we would be able to achieve the ultimate Trifecta of Victory – we would have completed The Free Shelby Plan, The Expedition to Blue Cave Plan and The Rescue Annabelle Plan all before Shelby's parents discovered that she had ditched summer school!

But this wasn't the movies.

CHAPTER TEN: RECKONING

It's always the little details. When Jacques flung Nar off his shoulders, he and Crystal had no idea that such a small, insignificant action would have caused them to lose the Golden Sextant and ultimately get arrested by the Coast Guard. When I needed a substitute to pose for Shelby at Schooltastic! I never could have imagined that Puyat would be some type of freakish algebra-whiz. It's not that I didn't think Puyat was smart; it's that I didn't know the first thing about Puyat as she spoke only the Hmong dialect and I only spoke English.

Apparently (I found this all out later) Margaret

Folmsbee ended up really enjoying her lecture at Schooltastic! She even included a "class participation" section where she asked students to solve some problems using the Quadratic Formula (another thing I need to look up on Google). Some of the students were really stumped by Margaret's multi-variable questions, but not Puyat. She *breezed* through each and every one of them. Then Margaret decided that just for fun she would give the class a few of those "if a plane leaves Chicago travelling 300 miles per hour" word problems. Puyat was stumped. Not by the math, but by the English. Of course this drew the attention of the Banstons as neither Sid nor Sue remembered enrolling a non-English-speaking Hmong girl. Sid and Sue didn't really mind that a brilliant student in search of knowledge had been so enthusiastic about meeting Margaret Folmsbee that she crashed the lecture. What they *did* mind was discovering that their attendance count was off by one student. After taking the register, it became clear that the missing student was Shelby Ruiz. In fact, it almost seemed that the Hmong girl was attending the lecture *in place of Shelby Ruiz*. There was no way of confirming that with Puyat as no one in class spoke Hmong; so that's when Sid and Sue made the call to Mrs Ruiz.

Mrs Ruiz then called her husband, who was in the middle of teaching his summer school class how to conjugate the irregular Spanish verb "estar". During their phone conversation about Shelby's disappearance, Mrs Ruiz's call-waiting beeped and when she switched over to the other line she found herself speaking to a counsellor from the Surf Island Elementary School Summer Camp who was reporting that their other daughter, Annabelle Ruiz, had somehow been "lost" after snack time. Mrs Ruiz did not panic *only* because she was absolutely *certain* that her two daughters' disappearances were connected. When she clicked back to the other line, this was exactly what she explained to Mr Ruiz. He didn't panic either. He knew exactly what he was going to do the moment he hung up the phone with his wife – he was going to call my father.

My dad thought Shelby was a "terrific, terrific kid" (his words, not mine). He naturally assumed that Mr Ruiz felt the exact same way about me. That's one of my dad's best qualities; he doesn't notice a lot of stuff that goes on. So when my dad got the call from Mr Ruiz, he just thought it was one concerned father calling another to find out what mischief their kids might have gotten into. My dad had no idea that Mr

Ruiz thought I was some kind of human "bolt cutter", who wanted to sever the "links of the chain" that connected Shelby to her future at a great university. My father told Mr Ruiz not to worry. He knew that I was planning to head out for Blue Cave and naturally assumed that Shelby had gone with me. My dad also theorized that Shelby had taken Annabelle along on the journey, maybe to buy her silence. He actually thought Mr Ruiz would be kind of "amused" that Shelby had ditched summer school and Schooltastic! In my father's mind, kids did this type of thing every day; it wasn't that big a deal. Why, when he was younger, my dad had done the same kind of things. That's why my father was so *shocked* at Mr Ruiz's reaction. Mr Ruiz *demanded* that my father meet him in the parking lot of Schooltastic! (Mr Ruiz was a very smart man; he knew we would try to get Shelby back to Schooltastic! before 7 P.M.). Mr Ruiz wanted to make sure my father would "straighten me out" and stop me jeopardizing Shelby's future by "coercing" her into "truancy". Even after hanging up the phone call my father just thought that Mr Ruiz was having a bad afternoon and was certain that deep down he thought that I was a "terrific, terrific kid". He was sure Mr Ruiz didn't mean it when he had said, "We have to put an end to this Outriders nonsense once and for all." By the time my father had opened the door to his Surf Island Signs pickup truck, Mr Ruiz had already called:

1. Bettina's parents, Mr and Mrs Conroy, at The Cut Hut, the salon they run on Surf Island Boulevard.

2. Ty's dad, Mr Dyminczyk, who was driving in his TOSIWD (Town of Surf Island Water Department) truck after having repaired a water main.

3. Din and Nar's parents, Tran and Lin Bonglukiet, who had been working the counter at Surf News, their small market. Actually, one of the Bonglukiet cousins took the call and translated Mr Ruiz's message into Thai.

4. Wyatt's parents, Morgan and Betty Kolbacher, who then reported to Mr Ruiz that their twin purple Yamaha WaveRunners they had reported stolen had been spotted by the Coast Guard Station in Cedar Cape being driven by three kids whose description closely matched those of Wyatt, Shelby and Cam.

This last bit of news sent shockwaves through the entire group of parents; particularly the additional detail that the two personal trainers who had their office up in The Bluffs, Jacques and Crystal Requin, had been arrested for piracy, boat theft, grand larceny and possibly attempted *kidnapping*. A Coastie was kind enough to forward a strange video-clip phone message they had received showing Annabelle Ruiz chomping down on the finger of an unknown woman with a hammerhead shark tattoo. After a series of cell phone calls among all the parents, full scale PANIC had overtaken the group.

Of course Shelby, Wyatt and I had no idea all this inter-parental communication had transpired when we beached the two purple Yamahas at Rocky Point and headed over the dunes towards Schooltastic! Shelby had the blue duffle on her shoulder; inside was the Golden Sextant. Annabelle was safe and sound with Ty, Din, Nar and Howie. Life was good. We were convinced we had gotten away with all of it. In fact, we were so positive of this that we planned to meet up later at Island Freeze to down a bunch of SurfFreezes so we could celebrate.

Our first inkling that something was terribly, terribly wrong was seeing Mr and Mrs Ruiz, Mr and Mrs

Bonglukiet, Mr and Mrs Conroy, Morgan and Betty Kolbacher, Mr Dyminczyk and my dad in the parking lot of Schooltastic! I'm pretty sure it was the first time that all the parents of The Outriders had been together in the same place at the same time but I couldn't really concentrate on that because I was distracted by the police cars. And the huge black Rolls Royce.

Apparently (I found this out later) Mr Thorpe's video surveillance system covered every inch of his estate. He had a full-colour high-definition digital video recording of Shelby scavenging the Golden Sextant which he had apparently shown to the entire Surf Island Police Department because there were FOUR squad cars flanking Mr Thorpe's Rolls Royce. So by the time Shelby, Wyatt, and I cut through the small scrubby grove of pines near the dumpster behind Island Pangs, we realized that we had stepped into level ten on the expert setting of DOOM. There were so many of *them* and so few of *us* that clearly we were headed for certain annihilation. If only Puyat hadn't been such a freakish algebra-whiz.

Mr Ruiz looked like he was about to *explode* with rage. His face was turning a purple colour that reminded me of the Yamaha. He was looking at

Shelby as if they were the only two people in the parking lot and there weren't like twenty other people standing around. Mr Ruiz let loose with a tirade of Spanish. I felt lucky I had no idea what he was saying (the words "wave" and "surfboard" never came up) but it was absolutely, perfectly clear, even to the Bonglukiets, that Mr Ruiz was in a region *way* past anger in the white-hot zone of rage. Shelby was so unprepared for this ambush that it looked as if someone had hit her on top of the head with a frying pan.

Two things saved us. The first was Howie's bark. Lin Bonglukiet fed Howie, so each time Howie saw Mrs Bonglukiet he would bark, hoping to remind her that his massive 243 pound body needed food. Howie's bark was so incredibly deep and loud that it caused everyone in the Schooltastic! parking lot to turn in his direction. As Howie bounded over to Mrs Bonglukiet, we all saw Din, Nar, Bettina, Ty and of course *Annabelle* enter the parking lot. Annabelle looked just as she always did, perfectly groomed, her school uniform still a bit wet, but otherwise unharmed. A wave of RELIEF washed over the parents as they all swarmed towards Annabelle led by Mr and Mrs Ruiz. For a moment, no one was paying any attention to Shelby, Wyatt and me. Bettina, Ty, Din and Nar circled along the edge of the parking lot and joined us near the dumpster.

Nar leaned close to me and whispered, "Howie saved us."

I put my arm around Nar's shoulder and said, "Howie is a hero."

Nar nodded. He had known this all along, but was glad the rest of us finally knew too.

All of us knew, without saying anything further, that our reprieve from the mob's attention would only be temporary. It actually only lasted about three seconds, until a chauffeur opened the door to the Rolls Royce and helped Mr Thorpe into a standing position on the asphalt of the parking lot. Eight policemen formed a semi-circle around the group of us; as if a bunch of 12-year-olds planned to make a run for it and become fugitives from the law.

Immediately Shelby unzipped the blue duffle and pulled out the Golden Sextant. She handed it to Mr Thorpe.

"We didn't steal it. Again."

"I know," Mr Thorpe said as he took the sextant from Shelby. He barely glanced at the priceless artifact it to see if it had been damaged.

"But . . ." was all I could think to say.

"It didn't make sense – first you *return* the sextant and then you *steal* it back?" Mr Thorpe said, once again reading my thoughts.

"Yeah, but . . ." Shelby said as she pointed to all the police.

"I thought you must have been in danger," Mr Thorpe said.

"Oh," Wyatt said.

We were all relieved to find out we weren't being arrested. But by now all of the Outrider parents had swarmed back in our direction. Mrs Ruiz was carrying Annabelle in her arms, not willing to let her go even for a second. Mr Ruiz stepped forward to confront Shelby, but before he could get a word out of his mouth, Mr Thorpe said to him, "You should be extremely proud of your daughter and her friends. They were in a tough spot and they handled it as well as anyone could have."

"Thank you, Chappy," Shelby said as if she and Mr Thorpe hung out at Island Freeze all the time.

Now Mr Ruiz looked like someone had hit *him* with a frying pan. He had been all prepared to go after Shelby, but after Mr Thorpe made his comment it was as if the wave of anger died out from under him. Then Mr Thorpe shook all of our hands.

When he got to me he leaned close to my ear and whispered, "Now you owe *me* one." Mr Thorpe had been the second thing that saved us – and somehow he knew it. That kind of freaked me out but it also made me respect and fear Mr Thorpe more than anyone else I had ever met.

Then "Chappy" had his chauffeur help him into the Rolls Royce and the black car glided away, the police escort trailing behind it.

DIME CON QUIEN ANDAS, Y TE TIRÉ QUIEN ERES.

Mr Ruiz reached out his hand for Shelby and said, "We're done here."

Shelby didn't take her father's hand. She said, "But *I'm* not done."

"Excuse me?"

"We're all going to Island Freeze."

"I don't think so." Mr Ruiz took Shelby's hand. Shelby pulled it away.

"And I'm not going back to summer school or Schooltastic!"

There were a lot of people crowded around Mr Ruiz and Shelby and none of them said a word. Mr and Mrs Bonglukiet looked to Din and Nar for a translation; the twins each held up their hands as if to say, "not now".

"We'll talk about this at home."

"It doesn't matter where we talk about it. I'm not changing my mind."

Mr Ruiz gestured towards me and the rest of our group. "You've let them influence you."

"This isn't about my friends. This is about *me*."

"You're too young to know anything about you."

All of a sudden Mrs Ruiz stepped forward. Annabelle was still in her arms. "Armando, what would you hope your daughter values more – straight A's or friends that would risk their lives for her?"

All my life I believed that Mr and Mrs Ruiz acted as a single parental unit. I never suspected that Mrs Ruiz might have found Mr Ruiz kind of irritating just like I did.

No one was more surprised than Mr Ruiz. He opened his mouth to speak but no words came out.

"The good thing is Shelby has both – straight A's *and* friends that would risk their lives for her!" I said and immediately regretted having opened my mouth. Even Mrs Ruiz who was taking Shelby's side glared at me – I had waded into waters I had no business swimming in.

"We're going to Island Freeze, Mando, I hope that you will join us."

Mrs Ruiz reached out her hand for Shelby. Then she, Shelby and Annabelle walked through the parking lot, all the other families clearing a path for them. Mr Ruiz gave me a hard stare, then turned and followed his family.

My dad came over and kind of tousled my hair. "You OK?" he asked.

"Yeah," I said.

"Good story to tell me?"

"Ultra-good."

"Looking forward to it," Dad said, without a whole bunch of enthusiasm.

"Can we go to Island Freeze with Shelby? I'm starving."

"Think of it as your last supper."

"Grounded?"

"Absolutely."

"Think Shelby will be?"

My dad looked around at all The Outriders and said, "I think it will be the mother of all groundings."

And so it was. Shelby, Wyatt, Bettina, Din, Nar, Ty and I didn't see each other for about three weeks. Well, at least our parents didn't *think* we did. But

Shelby didn't have to go back to summer school or Schooltastic! Mr Ruiz even stopped threatening to send her to boarding school. Even though the Banstons lost a paying student, they were kind enough to give Puyat a scholarship to learn English and hired her as an enrichment counsellor for the algebra students. The rest of the summer went by kind of quickly. We had a few more expeditions but of course none of them lived up to the hugest, most dangerous, and ultimately coolest thing that ever happened to us. That is, until we headed out on the Expedition to Willow Key. But I'll get to all that stuff later.

Signing off:

THE OUTRIDERS BLOG

EXPEDITION: BLUE CAVE
Entry by: Cam Walker

TURN THE PAGE FOR A SNEAK PEEK AT THE OUTRIDERS' NEXT ADVENTURE . . .

CHAPTER ONE: HARVESTING

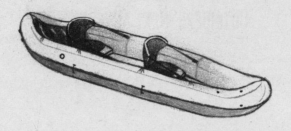

I was breaking every safety rule of scuba diving. I wasn't certified or even junior certified, which is what someone my age needs to be. I was diving at dawn in murky, unfamiliar waters, and worst of all, I was diving *alone*. The number one hugest mistake you can make when you strap on a scuba tank is to go into the water without a diving buddy. You'd think that I would have been freaked out, but I wasn't. The only thing I was worried about was that someone might spot me, because I definitely shouldn't have been swimming in the water hazard that fronted the seventh green of The Bluffs Country Club.

Most of the members of The Bluffs Country Club are old – really, really old. There is a reason for this. It costs a ton of money to join The Bluffs, and on top of that the members don't just let "anyone" join. You have to be the "right sort" of person. So I guess if you want to play golf at The Bluffs it takes a long time to save up the money to join the club, and then it takes even longer to convince people that you are "member material". This must take around sixty years, because most of the guys that tee it up have hearing aids and those ultra-thick glasses that old dudes wear.

I don't know much about golf, but I do know that guys who are really, really old have a tough time reaching the seventh green, which (according to a sign on the tee box) is 210 yards long.

On the plus side, most of these ancient guys can't see or hear when their golf balls plunk into the water hazard in front of the green, which is why there are *thousands* of barely used balls resting at the bottom of the small pond, just waiting to be harvested.

Each used golf ball is worth twenty-five cents to Chuck at Surf Island Discount Golf and Tennis. So you can understand why golf ball farming is *critical* to funding the expeditions of the Outriders and why

I was scuba diving alone in front of the seventh green.

Well, I wasn't exactly alone. My friend Wyatt Kolbacher and I had scavenged two Bluffs Country Club golf carts and he was hiding a few dozen yards away in the woods. Many years ago, when we were in fifth grade, Wyatt made a breakthrough discovery that has revolutionized transportation for the Outriders. All golf carts are started with a small key. It was Wyatt who realized that all of the golf carts at The Bluffs use *the exact same key*. If you have a key for one of the carts, you have a key for them all. So, of course, each of us had our *own* key, which comes in really handy when you need to transport more golf balls than you can carry.

On a normal golf ball farming excursion Wyatt and I wouldn't bother scavenging two golf carts. We also wouldn't risk something as dangerous as scuba diving in a water hazard. We would simply harvest the balls that had zinged off into the woods (which for some reason, the members call "the rough"), slip them into our backpacks, and then duck under the "guest entrance" we had created in the perimeter fence that surrounds the country club. From that point we would hook the backpacks to a trolley pulley that we had rigged to a zip line. The zip line connects the highest point in Surf Island, The Bluffs, with the lowest point, The Flats, where all of my friends and I live. Once the backpacks had whooshed down the zip line through the pine trees they would end up at the Good Climbing Tree in my best friend Shelby's backyard. Shelby would climb the tree (she's ultra-gymnastic), unhook the backpacks, and store the balls in an old barrel we call "the Ball Barrel".

But this wasn't a normal day of golf ball farming. We had to finance a HUGE expedition (don't worry, I'll tell you about it later) so we needed to take even HUGER risks.

I had just finished filling up my fifth backpack full of balls when I heard a *plunk*. The plunking noise didn't sound like a fish jumping *out* of the water or a frog jumping *into* the water. It sounded like a golf ball landing very close to my head, and that's when I realized two things:

1. Golfers get up freakishly early to play golf.
2. I was going to be spotted.

Sure, I could have stayed underwater and hoped that the four elderly Bluffs members wouldn't spot a twelve-year-old scuba diving in the water hazard. But even though I wasn't certified or junior certified as a diver, I was experienced enough to read my compressed air gauge, which was very close to empty. Also, even if I managed to avoid this foursome of golfers, there was sure to be more of them following close behind.

Even though the guys playing golf had those really thick old-guy glasses, they had no trouble spotting a kid in a wetsuit, flippers, and scuba tank crawling out of the water hazard and onto the seventh green. I didn't know exactly how long it would take them to get into their carts and zoom the 210 yards towards me, but they did move a lot faster than I expected.

I yanked the scuba fins off my feet, picked up the backpack full of balls, and sprinted across the green into the woods where Wyatt was hiding. I could hear the angry golfer dudes jumping out of their carts and heading towards our position. I tossed the BC (buoyancy compensator) vest, mask and fins into Wyatt's golf cart and then jumped into mine. Wyatt could tell by how fast I was moving exactly what was going on. He could have said, "Wow, you set the all-time record for golf ball farming!" Or he might have said, "You are freakishly brave!"

But instead, Wyatt chose to say, "I told you that last dive was one too many."

Wyatt has a peculiar talent for sometimes saying the exact thing you don't want to hear.

"We absolutely needed the golf balls," I said.

"We absolutely needed not to be caught."

It was hard to argue with the truth, so I just jammed my foot down on the accelerator pedal and rocketed the golf cart *right back towards the seventh green*.

One thing I can say for sure, the angry golfer dudes did not expect to see the trespassing kid in the wetsuit blasting out of the woods and heading straight back *at them*. I could tell it didn't make any sense to the foursome because they all froze for a few seconds trying to figure out how I could possibly be so insane as to drive *towards* trouble instead of *away* from it. Since they were still on foot, I zipped right through the frozen foursome, spraying them with pine needles. After that, they didn't stay immobile for long. All of them started yelling at the top of their lungs for me to stop (as if) and then scrambled towards their carts. But in the time it took for them to get their golf carts in gear, I was a few hundred yards down the fairway cruising towards the clubhouse.

One thing *I* didn't expect was for the guys chasing me to use their cell phones and call in reinforcements. I didn't actually turn around and see them make the calls. I just figured it out because the next thing I saw was a squadron of golf carts rising over the hill just to the left of me. It kind of reminded me of one of those Xbox 360 games when you have just cleared a dungeon of a bunch of mutants and then you go through a doorway and there's like 150 new mutants waiting to rip your head off.

You would think I would have employed some kind of evasive manoeuvre and tried to outrun the ten golf carts that were now chasing me. But I didn't do that. I kept heading straight for The Bluffs clubhouse. Once again, my odd strategy confused my pursuers. They had so expected me to veer *away* from them that some of them had *anticipated* my move and made turns in the direction they *thought* I was going to go. This caused a few of the golf carts to collide and in the confusion I was able to jet ahead over a small rise where I could see the McGooghan Bridge in front of me.

The McGooghan Bridge, which according to a brass plaque mounted on the handrail was named after some Scottish guy who designed the course in

1803, is really narrow. It is wide enough for only one golf cart to go across at a time. If you were playing a normal round (and weren't being chased by twenty angry guys) you would tee off at the first tee right next to the outdoor patio of The Bluffs clubhouse, drive across the McGooghan Bridge, and head out to the first fairway. But I was now doing the exact opposite – I was careening towards the narrow bridge and planning to drive across it in the wrong direction.

The golfers chasing me must have been pretty amused at my choice of escape route, because I could hear them laughing. It was hard to blame them, as I could see a colourful wall of ancient golfers wearing pink and green pants, white-coveralled caddies, green-uniformed groundskeepers, golf course marshals wearing blue jackets, red-vested valet parkers, black-aproned waiters, and grey-shirted locker room attendants lined up on the clubhouse side of the bridge, just waiting for me to cross so they could capture me, bring me to justice, and ship me off to a youth authority work camp where I would be wearing some kind of orange jumpsuit. But there were three things they all didn't know:

1. The backpack next to me contained no farmed golf balls – only crumpled up newspapers.
2. By this time Wyatt had sent all five backpacks (which *were* stuffed with farmed golf balls) down the zip line.
3. I was never going to make it to the other side of McGooghan Bridge.

The narrowness of the bridge worked to my advantage. No one wanted to risk a head-on collision with a psycho kid in a wet suit, so everyone on the clubhouse side just held their position. The old and angry golfers behind me had now spread out and thought they were *herding* me towards the narrow bridge. I raced onto the fairway side of the bridge, and since there was no possible way to turn around, the guys chasing me simply stopped their carts and waited so they could enjoy the show of me getting captured near the clubhouse. Halfway across I skidded to a stop and without hesitating even a millisecond, I JUMPED OVER THE RAILING of the McGooghan Bridge.

I know, it sounds kind of Tom Cruise-like and dangerous, but the McGooghan Bridge is only about fifteen feet high and I knew *for sure* I was going to land in a soft grassy spot. I knew this because a few hours earlier I had scouted this escape route. That's why I chose that exact spot to hide the inflatable canoe.

The Bluffs Country Club is affiliated with the Bluffs Yachting and Beach Club. I only mention that because the Yachting and Beach Club was a deep resource for scavenging all types of nautical craft – like the inflatable canoe. Not many ultra-ancient dudes can paddle an inflatable canoe. But for some strange reason the members of the Y & B Club all own either kayaks or canoes (they also own huge sailboats and motor cruisers, but that has nothing to do with my story). I was pretty sure that the lawful owner of the canoe was probably one of the old guys yelling at me from the McGooghan Bridge, but I was also pretty sure that the owner would never in a million years recognize the bright yellow boat as something that he had bought and paid for. So I had scavenged the canoe, knowing full well I was going to return it after escaping down the Puerta River.

The Puerta River is more like a raging brown stream. But it was plenty big enough for the inflatable canoe to navigate. It's fast moving, particularly after rain, and as soon as I pushed the yellow boat into the current, I was racing down the Puerta, leaving about fifty angry golfers and about the same number of country club staff behind me. I could hear their shouts echoing in the narrow granite ravine that held the Puerta. But the ping-ponging shouts became softer and softer as the current took me away from the country club.

I promise I'm not bragging, but my plan had worked really well. That's kind of what I'm best at – planning stuff. I'm not like one of those kids you read about who dream up a scheme to link up a bunch of computers and find a way to win at Internet poker (really happened), but when it comes to figuring out a way for The Outriders to go on cool expeditions and getting the gear we need, I'm ultra-good. Which is why I was so surprised when the waterfall came up on me so quickly.

Of course I *knew* about the waterfall. What I didn't know was how strong the current just above the falls can be. I had planned to navigate the canoe to a calm section of the river created by an enormous fallen pine. But now I realized my canoe and I had whipped past the small inlet and no amount of paddling on my part was going get me out of the churning rapids that were funnelling me directly towards the falls.

I feel really comfortable on fast-moving water. I surf. I surf a lot. So it wasn't like I was panicking. In fact my mind was clear and clicking through all my possible options:

1. Jump out of the canoe.
2. Stay in the canoe.

Unfortunately both option one and option two had the same end result: I was going over Puerta Falls. I made a split-second decision to stay in the canoe. A few months back I had tried diving off some cliffs (not huge ones like you see on SKY Sports). I came out of one of my dives and landed a little more horizontally than vertically. And it hurt – really badly. So my thinking was that the bright yellow boat was *inflatable* and my body was *not*, so I thought I'd let the canoe absorb as much of the impact as it could stand. Also – and this proved to be faulty reasoning on the part of my brain – I thought that if I was *in* the canoe with my paddle, maybe there was some way for me to *navigate* down the falls.

Here's an important thing to remember if you ever find yourself in a similar situation:

- An inflatable canoe falling over a waterfall tends to act like a sail and lift the boat AWAY FROM THE WATER and into the AIR.

So none of my surfing or paddling experience was going to come into play. I was free-falling, and most frightening of all (I'll admit I was now ultra-scared) the canoe *folded* in half and I was swallowed in a yellow cocoon of polyvinyl fabric. I couldn't see or hear a thing. I didn't know if I was going to land in the crash pool of the waterfall, or splatter against the boulders that ringed the pool. For some reason Wyatt's voice popped into my head. His voice said, "The plan wasn't so good after all."

Wyatt's voice disappeared as soon as I heard the explosion. Well, it wasn't really an explosion – it was the sound of the inflatable canoe smacking into the crash pool and rapidly DEFLATING. The next thing I knew I was deep underwater, tangled in the now limp yellow canoe and struggling for a way to claw myself out of the wreckage and make it to the surface. Picture putting a roll of quarters inside of a napkin and throwing it into the water; the napkin would fold up around the quarters and sink straight to the bottom. I was now the roll of quarters and the deflated boat was the napkin.

I remembered Wyatt showing me a movie about U.S. Navy Seals. In one of the training scenes, the Seals get dunked upside down in a deep pool. Their super-tough drill instructor tells them to follow the air bubbles to the surface. That seems like a really terrific survival technique, especially in a swimming pool where you can see the bubbles. But here in the deep dark depths of the crash pool, I couldn't see any bubbles. Not one bubble. But, like I said, I'm at home in or around the water, so I did finally claw my way out of what was left of the yellow canoe and find my way to the surface. I then took the biggest inhale of fresh air my lungs could hold. Apparently at some point I must have been screaming, because I needed to take in a lot of air.

About now you must be wondering, *were the golf balls really worth it?* The answer is no, but the expedition to Willow Key absolutely was. I guess you'll have to read my blog to find out the whole story. . .

OUTRIDERS: EXPEDITION TO WILLOW KEY

Cam Walker and his friends are off on a field trip to Willow Key. But amid the usual school dramas, the Outriders get enmeshed in a much bigger 'field trip' than they had ever planned. The thick marsh is good at concealing alligators, but it's even better at hiding drainage pipes taking run off from a big resort development. There's also the small matter of a second artefact that leads them back to a most unexpected Surf Island resident. Suddenly the field trip gets a whole lot more exciting!

ISBN: 1416926720 £5.99 pbk
ISBN-13: 9781416926726

ED DECTER

OUTRIDERS

Expedition to Pine Hollow

Eagle Tower is just about the most important place in the world to Cam Walker and his friends. The first Outrider expedition ever was a hike to Eagle Tower. In fact, it's where they became Outriders. So when they find out that a mining company is going to tear the tower down in five days time, the Outriders decide to plan one last expedition there. But, as usual, things don't go exactly as planned when the mining company starts dynamiting five days ahead of schedule, and one of the Outriders is keeping an important secret...

ISBN: 1416926739 £5.99 pbk
ISBN-13: 9781411926733

TIME RUNNERS: FREEZE-FRAMED

At first, Jamie Grant thinks people are just ignoring him. His teacher, his classmates, even his own mother – everyone apart from his little sister, Ellie – are suddenly acting as if he's not around. He's fallen off the register at school, people don't reply to his questions, and he's not even showing up in old family photos.

With the help of the mysterious Anna, Jamie comes to realise that he doesn't exist. He never has. He's fallen through a time break and is living in a parallel world in which he was never born. But Jamie soon discovers that although he is outside time, he has the power to control it – and so he and Anna are employed as Time Runners to fix the rips in time. But they must work against the sinister Darkling Midnight, who is intent on causing chaos throughout history, to prevent time from falling apart...

ISBN: 1416926429 £5.99 pbk
ISBN-13: 9781419626429

TIME RUNNERS: REWIND ASSASSIN

It's 1596, and Time Runners, Jamie and Anna, have been sent on a mission to fix the rips in time and prevent time from falling apart. In sixteenth century London they encounter a man dressed in a modern suit, carrying a sniper rifle, planning an assassination. And the chief candidate seems to be leading playwright William Shakespeare. Sinister Darkling Midnight, surrounded by menacing skitters, claims to want to form an alliance with the Time Runners, but can he be trusted?

As the Spanish Armada, wrecked and defeated eight years previously, surfaces in the Thames, zombie-like drowned sailors and soldiers leap ashore to invade London. Jamie and Anna will need all their ingenuity and all of Jamie's emerging power over time itself to defeat the Armada yet again and thwart Midnight's dastardly plans.

ISBN: 1416926437 £5.99 pbk
ISBN-13: 9781416926436